This was his revenge made real.

But it wouldn't do to gloat. Leontina Tavian was not what he'd expected at all—not that night after the wedding and not today—and that was going to take some getting used to.

Right now, what he could not do, because it would cause undue chaos in his own life—and Pau did not allow his life to be messy, ever—was to let her know that he'd planned all this from the beginning. He had sought her out, seduced her and had kept going all night long in the hope of this precise outcome.

He could not let her see that this was a victory, not today. Not yet.

"I suppose it doesn't matter," he said, after some while. Then his gaze found hers and held, and he could not seem to control the intensity in his voice, then. "Because if you are carrying the heir to Calixto Enterprises—if you are carrying *my child*—then I fear, Leontina, that the only man you will marry is me."

The sparkling new duet by
USA TODAY bestselling author Caitlin Crews!

A Very Italian Scandal

The Tavian siblings are always front-page news!

Giaco and Leontina Tavian are no strangers
to scandal—it's their hateful father's main legacy!
But they're both about to make headlines
for the most unexpected of reasons…

When legendary playboy Giaco agrees to a convenient
marriage with his deliciously disapproving stepsister Ivy,
he never expects that the biggest scandal of all will be
his own uncontrollable need to claim her for real…

You won't want to miss the drama of
To Have & To Hate

Reserved Leontina has always avoided the limelight…
until her secret baby bombshell is revealed!

Enjoy *Revenge Paid in Pregnancy*

Both available now!

REVENGE PAID IN PREGNANCY

CAITLIN CREWS

PRESENTS

Recycling programs for this product may not exist in your area.

ISBN-13: 978-1-335-21389-1

Revenge Paid in Pregnancy

Harlequin Enterprises ULC
22 Adelaide St. West, 41st Floor
Toronto, Ontario M5H 4E3, Canada
www.Harlequin.com

HarperCollins Publishers
Macken House, 39/40 Mayor Street Upper,
Dublin 1, D01 C9W8, Ireland
www.HarperCollins.com

Printed in Lithuania

1 2 3 4 5 6 7 8 9 10 LIT 28 27 26 25

USA TODAY bestselling, RITA® Award–nominated and critically acclaimed author **Caitlin Crews** has written more than one hundred and thirty books and counting. She has a master's and PhD in English literature, thinks everyone should read more category romance and is always available to discuss her beloved alpha heroes—just ask. She lives in the Pacific Northwest with her comic book–artist husband, is always planning her next trip and will never, ever read all the books in her to-be-read pile. Thank goodness.

Books by Caitlin Crews

Harlequin Presents

Greek's Christmas Heir
Her Accidental Spanish Heir
Forbidden Greek Mistress
An Heir for Christmas
Sicilian Devil's Prisoner
King's Heir of Hate

Notorious Mediterranean Marriages

Greek's Enemy Bride
Carrying a Sicilian Secret

Work Wives to Billionaires' Wives

Kidnapped for His Revenge

A Very Italian Scandal

To Have & To Hate

Visit the Author Profile page
at Harlequin.com for more titles.

CHAPTER ONE

WHEN HER FATHER shifted from making vague threats about one day marrying her off to the unpleasant, yet undefined, man of his choosing into concrete plans involving dinner dates and a selection process among a set of specific suitors, Leontina Tavian understood that it was time to escape.

At last.

What shocked her was that even though she'd known all along that this would happen and had worked out a plan to address this situation the very moment she determined that her condition could no longer be hidden, it still managed to shock her that the moment itself had arrived.

In the form of the person least likely to notice any changes in her, because he barely saw her.

Her father did not skulk about, much less sneak, and therefore could not possibly know what Leontina's plans were. Much less why she'd had to make them.

And yet here he was, filled with his usual bluster.

She'd been minding her own business in the family castle—though, really, the castle was nothing more than a monument to her father's boundless self-regard—

reading in the library. The library where, she'd been told, her late and long-lamented mother had spent the bulk of her time when she, too, had lived under Umberto Tavian's thumb.

This was only one reason the library was Leontina's favorite place in the castle. Another reason was that while she assumed from context clues that her father was literate, she had never actually *seen* him pick up a book in her life. And certainly none of the usual hangers-on who flitted all around him in the hopes he'd throw some of his money or influence their way could be accused of such a tedious pastime that could not possibly benefit their aspirations.

The library had always been Leontina's safe space. Since her father had not seen fit to pay any sort of attention to her education, she'd had to take matters into her own hands. Meaning that she had managed to read *almost* every book in this library, an enterprise that had taken her years. Particularly as some of the books in this library had clearly been placed here for aesthetics, not information or entertainment.

Still, one of the few things she knew about her late mother was that she had been a champion of education, and Leontina felt she had no choice but to try to follow in her footsteps. It was never a bad thing to have more knowledge rather than less.

Today, however, the footsteps that eventually disturbed her studies belonged—as unlikely as it seemed—to Umberto Tavian himself. Her father.

Who never, ever, came in here.

Or near her at all if he could help it.

Leontina was so startled that she almost gave him

the satisfaction of flinching when she looked up to see him standing there. He was scowling down at her as she sat in her favorite cozy chair, her feet propped up and a stack of books at her elbow.

"My God, you've turned out scraggly," was her only living parent's touching remark.

Umberto was not a nice man. He was not a kind man. It perhaps went without saying that he was also nothing in the broader neighborhood of a *good* man, either.

Unlike her older brother, Giaco, who liked to put on a show when in their father's presence, Leontina had always preferred to avoid the man entirely. Better to actually hide away, out of his sight, she'd always thought. Rather than what Giaco did, which was to parade about in plain and scandalous sight instead, thumbing his nose at their father at every opportunity.

But then, Giaco always had been the flashy one.

"Can I help you find a book to read?" she asked, because she couldn't imagine why else he was here. It was second nature by her twenty-fourth year to keep her voice neither too sweet—because that would set off her father's alarms, distrustful of *sweet* as he was, having no experience with it—or too deliberately bland, which would only enrage him.

Leontina liked to aim somewhere in between. It allowed her father to think that she was an idiot.

That he fully believed this, she was certain, was what had kept her safe for years.

"I'll need your appearance sorted out, and fast," he growled at her. Ignoring what she said, of course. "I've invited a selection of potential suitors for dinner tonight. You are to be entertaining, but not too bold. Demure, but not shy. Appealing, obviously, but nothing too tarty."

Leontina felt everything inside her go cold, though she knew better than to show it. She shook her head instead, as if she was confused. That was easy because she genuinely was confused.

"I'm sorry, but what sort of dinner party is this?" she asked, as if she hadn't heard the word *suitors*.

"The only point in having a daughter is marrying her off advantageously," Umberto barked at her. "How many times must I tell you this?"

She knew better than to answer the question. That drew undue attention, and Leontina's stock in trade was her ability to disappear. Right here in plain sight, if possible—though today he hadn't *happened upon* her. He'd come looking for her.

Her usual tricks weren't going to work.

"We have no choice but to make haste with this," Umberto continued in the same exasperated growl heavily laden with distaste, clearly not expecting her to answer him in the first place. It was the wise choice for a reason. "Your brother has ruined everything."

Leontina didn't know *exactly* what her infamous brother had done, only that it had driven her father utterly mad with rage. He'd come back from a business meeting in Madrid—the sort of thing he usually dominated and liked to brag about to his acolytes—in a grim fury.

According to the servants—who only dared whisper about their volatile employer in the deepest recesses of the castle where no one could hear them unless, of course, said *no one* was hiding in the wine cellars to avoid another spectacle at one of Umberto's endless dinner parties that were always filled with the worst sorts of people—Umberto had trashed half of his personal suite. Twice.

All while shouting Giaco's name.

This had left Leontina to attempt to solve the mystery of what her notoriously disreputable, scandalous brother could possibly have done to so well and truly get under their father's skin at last. The gloriously disgraceful Giaco Tavian was renowned far and wide for being the greatest waste of space that had ever assumed human form. That being the polite way to say that he was nothing but a fuck boy.

Leontina had long been under the impression that all her brother ever did was swan about from one exotic location to the next, gathering lovers as he went. It had been a great shock to her when he'd suddenly started dating her former stepsister, Ivy Amis, and then, even more astonishing, had married her. It had taken Leontina longer than she cared to admit to understand that it had been her father pulling those strings. Once she'd realized it, the unlikely romance between the Playboy of Positano—as Giaco had once been called after a particularly ribald holiday there that had resulted in his being escorted out to the city limits—and Saint Ivy of the Orphans—because despite her famous, late, film-star parents, Ivy really and truly did give all her time and money to orphans—made sense.

Umberto loved nothing more than to play puppet master over all and sundry. And especially if that all and/or sundry was Giaco, the son he'd expected would be made in his image who, instead, had made himself the greatest thorn in Umberto's side.

That was precisely why Leontina had taken matters into her own hands on the occasion of her brother's deeply surprising and unexpected wedding. It had been her only chance. She had been very clear on that going in. If her plan was to work, it had to work at that wedding. Any of the other ideas she'd come up with would raise her father's suspicions and likely get her locked away in a tower. The castle had three.

Luckily, that night had gone according to plan. It had gone much better than planned, in fact.

But she really needed to *not* think about that night, not now. Not while her father was staring at her, every line on his overindulged, always outraged body trembling with umbrage. She had to order herself not to let the instant wash of heat she felt when she thought about that night show on her face.

She had done what she needed to do. That was all that mattered. She had created an exit strategy and she'd simply been waiting these last few months— three whole months, to be exact—for some kind of sign. Something to make it clear that she had no choice but to put that exit strategy into immediate action.

Before the reason for the strategy took her over, that was, became impossible to conceal, and created even bigger problems for her.

And as her father stood before her, deliberately looming over her so she had no choice but to sit there quietly and gaze up at him as if in rapt attention, she knew the time had come. Because the men he started naming as his guests for the evening—the pack of would-be suitors handpicked by him because he believed they would give him more power and money, not because he gave one shit how his daughter would fare with any one of them—would have been appalling to her even if she hadn't already resolved to leave.

The youngest one was at least twice her age, she was fairly certain. And while Leontina had no quarrel with an age gap *in theory* as long as everyone involved was of sound mind and capable of consenting to it all, the men her father planned to parade her in front of tonight might as well have been crypt keepers.

She was fairly sure one of them actually *was* a crypt keeper.

But she nodded along as her father talked, as he laid out the benefits of each potential suitor and what there was to be gained from each one of them.

He meant *for him*. She knew that, of course. And if she hadn't known it already, this display from Umberto would have clued her in. If he was aware that she might have feelings about the person she was to marry, or might even have imagined he might solicit her input on this, he gave no sign.

That was just as well, she decided. Because Leontina's head was spinning. She fought to keep her pulse under control, because she had planned for this, *damn it*. She'd been planning how she would leave to avoid this very situation all along. But it was one thing to *imagine* what it would be like to finally know she had to leave this place at once—her childhood home, for good or ill, and the last place she'd seen her mother alive—and another to be *in that moment* at last.

Her father went on and on. He was ranting about

what the various suitors brought to the table but he was really talking about himself, of course. And when Umberto was done, when he finally wound himself down into little more than a few growls, he gestured at her impatiently.

"I can only imagine it will take you all afternoon to make yourself look presentable." When she didn't respond, he scowled. "But I warn you, Leontina. I will brook no opposition. If you do not have at least one marriage proposal by the end of the night, there will be consequences. Dire consequences. I hope you do not imagine that I am joking."

That seemed to require a response, so she ducked her head. Meekly, she hoped, though she'd always had trouble with that one. "I understand."

"I hope so, girl," Umberto snapped at her. "I hope so."

But then he left. And, like it or not, that meant it was time.

Leontina blew out a breath as the library doors closed behind him. Then she counted to ten—very slowly—just to make certain that he was really gone. Though he would have no reason to imagine she would do anything but obey him. She'd made certain of that through long years of work to keep herself as much beneath his notice as it was possible to get.

Still, she'd always known that this day would eventually come.

So she allowed herself that one, long breath. Then she launched herself into action, because she really had prepared for this.

She had spent years coming up with various ideas

on what constituted the best possible way to escape the castle. She'd had wild plans at first, no doubt cooked up after watching entirely too many summer blockbuster movies from America. Over time, she'd winnowed the plans down from over the top to something reasonable and practical instead.

In the end, she'd decided that simplicity was key.

She padded through the castle, taking the servants' stairs so that nobody would see her. Not that people really looked at her even if they did see her. Leontina had worked hard to make sure she was the sort of person everyone looked straight through. Still, there was always a chance that with her father on one of his rampages, someone could be hiding the same way she always did—but she didn't encounter a soul.

Leontina found her way to her rooms and gathered together the very few things she truly considered hers. Her mother's jewelry in a small velvet pouch. Just the handful of pieces that her mother had worn daily. She tucked them away and found her passport. Her laptop. Her wallet, which always contained a significant amount of cash as well as the single credit card she possessed in her own name. She'd had it since she was eighteen and had watched a documentary about escaping domestic violence. She had always kept the statements and bills digital and it was highly unlikely anyone even knew about it to question its use. Still, she was careful.

She took the time to conceal some items that she didn't want to leave, but couldn't take with her right now. Leontina had planned for this, too. She knew the castle better than anyone else, by virtue of hiding in it so often, and it was the work of only a few moments to secrete the things she didn't want anyone finding while she was gone. Because it was possible she would be gone for a very long time—she understood that. She hid her journals, and her mother's diaries, and a few other keepsakes in a secret hiding space behind an unremarkable panel in her dressing room.

There was no reason that anyone should push upon it. She knew this to be true because she'd hidden things there for years and no one had so much as disturbed the dust on it.

She took any personal items that it didn't make sense to carry with her tonight and put them there. And when she was done, she simply headed back down the stairs in the same outfit she'd been wearing earlier when her father had come upon her in the library, carrying nothing but a tote bag over her shoulder.

Leontina made it all the way down to the ground floor and then out one of the side doors without anyone noticing her. Once outside, she made her way directly to the garages, where she helped herself to one of the sets of keys that hung in a cupboard near the servants' door. She chose a car, set her bag on the passenger seat beside her, and with absolutely no fuss or carrying on, simply drove herself off her father's estate. The way she'd done hundreds of times before.

She even waved at her father's usual security detail as she passed through the gates at the bottom of the drive, and they waved back, because there was nothing remarkable in her driving off like this. She did it all the time. Even today, if security were to mention to her father that she'd done such a thing, she suspected that he might imagine she was sneaking off into one of the villages or even north toward Florence—where she could more easily please him with an item that was not a part of the wardrobe he liked to call *drab and uninspiring*, when he mentioned her attire at all.

That was simply the sort of obedience Umberto expected.

She hoped that was exactly what he thought. That she was off *pleasing* him while he plotted out the next, tragic chapter of her life to suit himself.

Meanwhile, she settled in and drove herself through the afternoon, into the evening, and on into France.

She spent that first night in Monaco in a busy, high-end hotel. Before she checked in, however, she sat in the well-appointed lobby, pulled out her laptop, and saw to a few housekeeping details. She changed all of her passwords. On everything, but particularly her bank and credit card accounts. Just in case anyone wanted to go looking once they realized she'd disappeared.

Umberto wasn't exactly known for his ability to let go.

Leontina ordered room service and then slept fitfully, with strange dreams of chase scenes and endless running waking her up repeatedly. It was very early when she decided she might as well get up and keep going. She spent a good eight hours on the road. She took the motorway that hugged the French coastline, following it all the way into Spain before she stopped in the outskirts of Barcelona.

And on the third day, she headed southwest and found her way into the rugged, terraced hillsides of Catalonia's Priorat region and one of its shining jewels, the Calixto estate.

There were hints of nobility and Romans alike in the family line, dating back centuries, but in more recent generations—meaning, since the monks left the area in the 1800s—the Calixtos had been all about wine. Leontina had read all about the family vintners and the ancient estate from every online source she could find—and there were a lot of them. Especially these days.

She knew she was in the right place not only because her GPS told her so, but because she saw the signs that led her straight toward the famous Calixto vines, stretching out in all directions like their own living history.

But it was only when she saw the great, sprawling house in the distance—clearly repurposed from some monastery back in the day, she was sure she'd read that somewhere—that she began to feel her nerves kick in.

Because she had done what she'd had to do. She would do it again. Leontina tried not to think too much about that night, and how…*shocking* it had all been. How *electrifying*.

How unprepared she'd found herself when all was said and done. Because it turned out, books did not in fact prepare a person for *everything*. Prepare them to *think* about it, perhaps. But to *do* it? Apparently not.

"A worthy lesson," she told herself now, trying to sound a bit hearty. Possibly even *jolly*.

As if she wasn't on her way to deliver a bombshell that might very well be poorly received.

In fact, she assumed it would be.

She blew out a breath as she drove and let one hand drop to smooth over her belly. It had been three months, almost to the day. She had never been one for communal dining when she could avoid it, so nobody had missed her when her relationship with food took a sour turn over the past few months. Leontina had become a kind of ghost in the kitchens because her cravings demanded one thing and nothing *but* that thing for several weeks, only to suddenly take against it the next.

She had only just begun to feel like herself again.

Just in time to move on to phase two, apparently. Which involved fewer cravings, she hoped. But was starting off with a whole lot more drama.

There had never been a possibility that she'd avoid that part. She'd known that, too.

She pulled up at what she assumed was the front door of the grand house and got out of the car. The drive had been beautiful, but as she stood there, breathing in the scent of a late September summer as it spilled over Catalonia, Spain, she felt the beauty of it all seem to…take her over. There had been signs of harvest all around as she'd driven through the region. The sky was so blue it ached, but the weather was mild and pleasant. It was tempting to relax, to imagine the worst was over. That she was safe now.

But when she closed the car door and turned toward the house itself, she froze.

Because *he* was standing there.

For a wild moment or two, she had the distinct impression that for the first time in her life, she might actually faint.

It was as if the earth and the sky kept changing places, but she realized it was in her head. Because *he* stayed exactly where he was.

He was none other than Pau Calixto. One of the wealthiest and most formidable men in Spain, and likely the world. Though she rather thought that was the least interesting thing about him.

The trouble with Pau was that he stole all the light from the sky and the sun as if it was his by right. And then kept it—because it was as if it all simmered there, beneath his skin, like a warning and an invitation at once.

She found herself breathless, and not for the first time.

He was very tall, with dark hair and fathomless dark eyes, and every part of him was lean and hard and commanding. His shoulders were broad and his hips were narrow and when she thought of him she always imagined him in a crisp, bespoke suit made in some or other dark fabric.

Even though today he wore only a pair of trousers and the sort of T-shirt that looked casual and likely rivaled the cost of the vehicle she was driving.

He did casual clothing as effortlessly as he did business attire. Leontina hadn't known that before now. It seemed a critical oversight on her part, because now there was no pretending that he didn't have one of the finest male forms she had ever beheld—and she had made a study of the male form, in fact. As a part of her education.

Surely that was what the internet was for, even in a mean old man's drafty castle.

But she looked up again and had to admit that despite the triumph of muscle and sinew that made him into something like art, it was his face that seemed to stake a claim deep within her. That stern, forbidding, uncompromising face.

She was already breathless, but that *face* made it worse.

Those dark eyes of his looked black from a distance but she knew, close up, that they contained threads of gold and the hint of green. He had a nose that made her think of predatory things—raptors, perhaps. Or great hawks. His mouth was stern and unsmiling, but the trouble was, she knew what he could do with it.

It felt like minimizing him to say that he was *beautiful*, because a word like that could not begin to contain him or describe him. It was too...soft.

When everything about this man was hard. Looking at him felt the way she imagined it would feel to be a bit of coal crushed down into diamonds.

And yet, just like on the day of her brother's wedding, she couldn't bring herself to look away from him.

Pau Calixto, the man who had ruined her father, according to the whispers in the cellars. The man who was in cahoots with her surprisingly devious brother, a shock to all, but especially to Umberto, who had imagined he was making a deal with Pau himself.

Pau Calixto, the man who was, though he didn't know it yet, the father of her baby.

Leontina forced herself to smile. She wished, suddenly, that she'd thought to pack something a little bit more elegant than the shapeless, serviceable dress she'd been wearing since leaving Tuscany.

But she couldn't do anything about that. There was only this.

Her exit strategy whether he liked it or not.

"Hello, Pau," she said, not exactly brightly. Though not, perhaps, as measured as she might have liked, either. "You might want to brace yourself. I'm afraid I've come with some potentially difficult news."

CHAPTER TWO

PAU CALIXTO COULD sift through probabilities the way regular humans processed the need to breathe—at lightning speed in a near-muscular response—and he could think of only one potential reason that this woman would be on his doorstep like this.

This particular woman at this specific time.

Clearly without anything like an invitation and by his count, a solid three months after he'd last seen her in the wake of her brother's wedding.

But he had not gotten anything in this world by getting ahead of himself.

Pau had received an alert that someone was approaching the house, having tripped the usual cameras. He had pulled up the feed and noted the vintage car with its Italian registration plate and had begun to draw conclusions based on that evidence alone. When he'd seen the woman behind the wheel, he'd felt a sense of triumph kick in—

Prematurely, he'd lectured himself.

That was ever a recipe for disappointment.

He'd made his way down to the front door, dismissing his hovering staff with a glance, because this was his project. This was his game to win or lose.

And Pau Calixto did not lose.

So all he did was go out and lean a bit in his doorway, here in this grand old folly of a house that his father had loved—perhaps more than he had ever loved another human, but Pau could not blame him for that. Not any longer.

After all, the old man had only ever had one friend in this life. And that had not exactly ended well for him.

"I thrive on difficult news," he told his best friend's younger sister, with the kind of calm that he knew could upend boardrooms full of peacocking billionaires who expected their big personalities to carry weight. "And had I known that you wished to visit me, Leontina, I would have extended an invitation. There can surely be no need to show up like this, so precipitously and without warning."

She was no peacocking billionaire, like her father—though Pau thought that Umberto's net worth had perhaps been downgraded quite a bit at this point. Umberto's daughter did not sputter and huff the way he would have done. All Leontina did was smile.

And Pau had made a small, personal study of that smile in the brief time he'd spent in her presence three months back. He had determined that it was practiced. Deliberate.

A tool she wielded, he'd decided. That made her smile the kind of game he could appreciate and admire.

A lot like the clothing she was wearing now. He had observed her for a few days before the wedding at her father's ostentatious castle, set down in the midst of the

Tuscan hills like someone had discarded it out of pique. She had dressed much like she was now, in shapeless pieces of clothing that she seemed to choose only from the ugliest possible shades, as if she was competing with herself to find the least flattering cut and color. Soon, he came to understand that she did it so that the eyes of her father and all of his self-important guests bounced right off of her.

He had gone to the wedding with the express purpose of meeting her, and so he had made a point of finding her in the midst of the festivities—something that had not been easy to do. He'd had to hunt her down—meaning, he found himself watching her during all the pompous events that Umberto had put on, all in an effort to celebrate himself rather than the happy couple.

Pau had watched the girl who seemed to be *trying* to disappear into the wall coverings. He'd watched as she'd now and again reacted to something someone was saying, usually Umberto or one of the guests like him. She had only showed the slightest flash of personality now and again, but he'd seen it. He'd noted it.

The roll of an eye. A checked sigh. A pursed lip, momentarily there and then gone.

He had also watched her shift back to become the wall itself, literally disappearing before the very faces of those who had elicited her tiny reactions in the first place.

It was like she was wearing an invisibility cloak that she could put on and take off at will.

More impressively, it worked.

He had been forced to acknowledge that if he hadn't been looking for her specifically, it might have worked on him, too. If he hadn't been determined to study her, he might have missed those moments that hinted at the real woman behind the shy and retiring act—because that's what he thought it was. An act.

If he hadn't decided in advance that he would seduce her, he would have missed her altogether—an indictment that Pau had not exactly been pleased with. But then again, when was the truth comfortable? That wasn't germane one way or the other. It was still the truth no matter how he felt about it.

Then, of course, there had been her attire at the actual wedding itself. When suddenly it was as if she'd found an entirely new wardrobe that she'd had secreted away somewhere the whole time, while she'd been shuffling around in rags instead. It was as if she was an entirely new woman, if only for the one day.

Like something out of a fairy tale, he thought now.

He had to remind himself that he was not a fanciful man. He was hardly one to tuck up with a book of fairy tales and glut himself on Cinderella stories—but the fact was, Leontina had *glowed*.

Her dark hair had spilled down all around her in thick waves, making her dark jade eyes gleam. It had been impossible not to see her then. Not only to *see* her, but to fully appreciate that the supposedly mousey and forgettable Leontina was, in every way, an heir to the same genetic cocktail that had made her brother one of the most sought-after men in all of Europe.

Simply put, Leontina was stunning. Mouthwateringly so, no matter how disconcerting he'd found it.

And once he'd seen it, he couldn't unsee it. Not even when she was up to her usual tricks, like today. She had her hair twisted severely back from her face and wore absolutely no makeup. If he didn't know better, he might think that her shape matched that of the dress she wore, because that thick, drapey fabric gave no hint of the body beneath it. All quite deliberate, he thought.

She even looked…rumpled. As if she hadn't slept well, and might possibly have tried to get a few hours' sleep in that shapeless sack she wore. She looked very much as if she'd been in this car for days.

He thought that perhaps she had been.

That, too, suggested that she was here for the precise reason he hoped she was.

But he could not permit himself to celebrate anything in advance. He could not allow himself to do anything but wait—as excruciating as that wait might have been.

He told himself it would be worth it. After all, as the saying went, if a man sat by a river long enough, the bodies of his enemies would float on by. It only took patience. Commitment. Dedication.

All things he was not only good at, but had long since perfected.

"Shall I tell you why I'm here?" she asked after a long moment. And though she sounded calm, he thought he saw a slight tremor move over her. That intrigued him almost more than the rest of her act did. "On your doorstep—and yes, regrettably, without an invitation?"

He didn't let himself react to the note in her voice that he doubted most ever heard. That hint of strength that he'd seen that night, but had second-guessed ever since. Perhaps he only wished that she was more sharp and tough than she seemed. Because that would make what he was doing less distasteful, surely.

Not that it mattered, he knew. He would do it either way.

The truth that Pau had spent these months coming to terms with, no matter what happened, was that he had set out to do exactly what he had done. It had not been a spur-of-the-moment idea. It had been a plan he had set out to execute, and had.

And while he could tell himself flattering fairy stories about *strength* and *inner resilience* on her part as he liked, the facts remained the facts.

He had deliberately set out to seduce his best friend's younger sister, at that same best friend's wedding, with one very precise goal in mind.

There would come a reckoning one day. This he did not doubt, because he knew his best friend. Sooner or later, Giaco would express his feelings on what Pau had done, and he doubted very much that he would enjoy what happened then.

But he could not allow himself to think of it. If he did, he would not move forward—and he had to move forward. His father deserved this justice, no matter what damage it would do to Pau and Giaco's friendship.

He shoved it out of his head.

And it didn't matter why Leontina was here today. His goal had either been achieved, in which case certain other steps would be put into motion. Or it had not been achieved, and if that was the situation, he would set about doing it all over again until his goal was within his grasp at last.

His body, he noted, did not view that possibility as any sort of chore.

But that was another truth he did not wish to examine. Not now.

He wondered if she could sense it all the same. If she knew the imperatives his body was issuing, somehow, because as she walked toward him—looking frumpy and delicious at once, as he was beginning to understand was her specialty—he thought he could see that awareness in her gaze.

That same awareness he had been so certain he'd seen all over her at the wedding.

Now, as then, he did not argue or explain or debate anything with her. He did not do such things, full stop. When Pau Calixto spoke, he made certain his words were received as pronouncements befitting laws.

Never *debates*.

He said nothing at all.

And Leontina took her time reaching him there at the doorway. He noticed she did not hurry either, and he liked that. These little hints of defiance pleased him, and not only because they suggested that she'd been precisely who he'd thought she was that night.

It astounded him how much he wanted that to be true. Even more so now that she was here. In Spain. On his land.

Here, something primal within him intoned. *At last*.

Pau wasn't sure he'd ever heard that voice before, but that didn't matter. What mattered was that it was right.

Once she climbed the wide steps to meet him, he still did not speak. He turned and led her into the grand old house that had once been a medieval monastery, though there had been, happily, some upgrades since.

A few months ago, he had led her into her father's oppressive castle, holding her by the hand as he'd led her through the typical warren of rooms until he'd found the suite that had been set aside for him. It had been lavish and over the top, as befit the partnership he'd been seemingly setting up with Umberto. He'd led her inside those rooms and he'd known that there was no chance whatsoever that anyone would disturb them before morning.

Pau had made great use of those hours.

The reality was that he would have done the same thing no matter who Leontina was or what reaction he'd had to her. That was the trouble with revenge—it had the potential to take more than it repaired. But it was who he was now. Pau had accepted this truth a long time ago.

Yet as he led Leontina into his own house this time, he was struck by another inconvenient truth—that he found this woman almost unbearably attractive, and more so now that she had come here. That she had sought him out, no matter her reasons.

That had not been part of his plan at all.

He could smell the subtle scent she wore, the suggestion of sea salt and honey. He could remember the taste of her cries and better yet, the way she had bucked her hips into his mouth, stretched out before him in total abandon.

Oh yes, he remembered everything about this woman.

He led her into one of the renovated sitting rooms,

done up to look modern and inviting, because these days the conversation between the medieval and the modern was all the rage. Or so his highly recommended and widely lauded architect and equally feted decorator had assured him. As long as the vineyards continued to make a profit and bolster his father's legacy, Pau didn't care what the old pile looked like.

Though he found the room greatly improved by the addition of Leontina. In short order, he had her seated neatly on a sofa while he sat opposite her, and then watched her too closely as his people brought in a few trays of local delicacies and various drink options.

"My thanks," she said, her eyes on the food set out on the low table before her, with no little flourish. "I am actually quite hungry."

"By all means, indulge yourself," he murmured.

He wasn't sure he meant to say that until he did. And when those dark jade eyes of hers flew to his, and the faintest hint of heat presented itself on her cheekbones, Pau understood that he'd meant to say it—and precisely the way he did.

It was exactly what he'd said when she'd wanted to return the favor that night. When she had crawled down the length of his body, settled herself between his legs, and licked him until he thought he might lose the plot completely.

Only to take him into her mouth and suck on him like some kind of dessert.

His body roared at him, but he prided himself on his intense control—no matter what it took. The only satisfaction he allowed himself was when her gaze dropped, yet her cheeks reddened further.

Because they were clearly recalling the same thing.

"You may recall the night of my brother's wedding," she said after she'd loaded up a small plate with some of the *pa amb tomàquet and la bomba*, and had eaten a bit.

Even watching her eat…affected him. "How could I forget?"

She shot him a swift glance, then dropped her gaze again. "What you may perhaps have forgotten is that we were rather…careless."

He had not forgotten. It had rather been the point of the exercise, at least going in, but he didn't say that. This was not the time to unveil every possible truth. Only some of them. Only the ones he knew he could use to his advantage.

And he had to remind himself not to assume he knew where this was going—though he did. He was certain that he did. The good news about that being that he could control his reactions well ahead of having anything concrete to react to.

Theoretically, anyway.

"I am not known for my carelessness," he said after a moment, as if he'd needed the time to sort through the reasons she might show up here and say such a thing.

Then he watched, fascinated, because she didn't fidget. She didn't twist her fingers around in her lap, bite her lower lip, or show any of the signs that he would have expected a woman in her position to exhibit. Instead, she seemed, if not perfectly at her ease, completely self-contained. Not scared or emotional or furious or any of the array of emotions he might have imagined she would be unable to hide.

It was fascinating.

"I'm pregnant," she told him. Straight and to the point, and he enjoyed that flare of victory deep inside him. Not to mention the immediate response from the cock that had gotten her in this predicament—and was clearly volunteering to continue its valorous service. "Before you ask, it's yours."

"Did you think I was unaware you were a virgin?" he asked.

He didn't mean to ask that either, though he was glad he had when the color grew on her face. It was the only sign she'd given so far that she was not as calm as she was pretending she was.

Because otherwise, all she did was aim that smile at him. That smile he knew was a *tool* she used. Meaning she was handling herself—and him. "My understanding is that paternity is always the first question when someone turns up with an announcement like this. Especially when the father is a man of your…" Her smile became something like demure, yet never quite reached her eyes. "Consequence, I think you'd call it."

Pau settled back against his chair. He studied her. He had been studying her for quite a while, though she couldn't know that, and yet he couldn't help feeling that somehow, he'd gotten it wrong. That he was missing something here, because she did not seem to be frantic over this.

That wasn't a bad thing, necessarily, but it wasn't what he'd expected.

And Pau Calixto did not generally like surprises. He preferred plans that were executed as expected. But then, Leontina had been a surprise from the start.

"I'm typically excellent at predicting behavior," he

told her after a moment that, this time, he had very much required. "And I would tell you that I would be deeply surprised indeed if, within three months, a twenty-four-year-old virgin who so as far as I'm aware very rarely leaves her father's home suddenly embarked upon a campaign of sin and scandal. Not that it couldn't happen. But I would think it would require more than one, single night of debauchery."

Leontina set her small plate down on the table between them. She seemed to take her time straightening. When she did, he could no longer see any color on her face and her gaze was cool.

He found himself even more intrigued than before.

"Was it debaucherous, then?" she asked, politely, as if inquiring after the time. "I didn't think it was, but then, as we've established, I have very little basis of comparison."

That sounded significantly spicier than he would have expected from her, especially in the absence of that weaponized smile. He felt something inside him sit up and take notice, and not simply because he would very much like to get his mouth on her again.

He was, regrettably, only a man.

"We barely slept," he reminded her, almost gently, though there was no denying the heat in his voice. He could see it reflected in her dark green gaze. "I had my mouth on every part of your body and you returned that favor. I took you in every position I could dream up. You came so many times you lost her voice." He shook his head. "How quickly they forget."

"Oh dear," she replied, her voice bland. *Too* bland,

he thought. "I didn't realize I was so special, Pau. I thought that was…just how it was."

Pau very nearly laughed at that. And that shocked him more than everything else that had come before. Who *was* this woman?

But there would be ample time to excavate that question. They just needed to come to terms—his terms.

"So you're pregnant," he said, and maybe he sounded a bit more serious than necessary. That was what happened when he nearly found himself *laughing* in the middle of what should have been a straightforward exchange of information. "I'm not surprised. It is perhaps easy enough to dodge one bullet. But we did not do it only the once, did we?"

Her smile reappeared then, and Pau could not decide if that was a victory or a loss.

"There is a rather more pressing issue than what I'm sure would be a delightful amble down memory lane," she said. He realized then that she was studying him, for a change. Or maybe it was that he was more aware of it now. "My father."

Her father.

Pau felt that same wash of fury and loathing take him over the way it always did at the very thought of the man. The vileness of Umberto Tavian had been the unifying glue between Pau and Giaco all these years. They had met at university and had become friends almost immediately. Back then, Pau had chafed at his father's restrictions much the way Giaco did, though he had not responded to those restrictions the way his friend had. Pau might have found his father's expectations stifling, but he knew that *his* father had operated—always—from a place of honor. That had made a difference.

So, too, had it made a difference that Pau idolized his father. Bernat Calixto had always seemed to Pau to epitomize all that a man was meant to be. As a child he might even have said that he loved his father, wildly, though he had quickly learned that such sentimentality was not welcomed.

His father might not have loved him. But he'd taught Pau to love the land, and that had been enough. Even today, he told himself that was enough.

He'd been fresh out of university when his father had died. An apparent heart attack, they told him. Bernat had simply keeled over in the midst of his beloved vines and, at first, Pau had accepted that. His father had loved this place above all else, as well he knew. Bernat had turned his own father's lackadaisical gesture toward the ancient winemaking capabilities of their land into an empire, and Pau had understood without it ever having to be explicitly stated that his father loved his varietals and his grapes more than he ever did his son.

Not that this was in and of itself a bad thing, to his mind. Because loving the wine was loving this land, and this land was their family's legacy. They were all bound to hold it and make it better, so that the Calixto name would not die out under their watch. Simply... *continue*. That was the requirement.

It was the least a Calixto heir could do, Pau had always thought. And maybe there was no better way for a man to love his son than to make it plain to him who he was and why it mattered that he grow up to honor the land that so many of his ancestors had toiled over across the centuries.

Pau had believed that. He had grieved, but he had accepted that he had been lucky enough not simply to chafe beneath his father's sense of honor, but to grow old enough to appreciate it.

It was not until he was going through his father's things in the aftermath of his death that he had discovered the truth. That Bernat had developed a deep, trusted friendship in his last years. Bernat had become a part of a particular group of European vintners, had become embroiled with their leader in a variety of ways, and had died with the full belief that he was about to lose everything that he built here.

The legacy of the Calixto family hung by a thread—and Bernat's sense of honor hinged on that legacy. On *continuing*.

The man he'd trusted had manipulated him there. Umberto Tavian. Rich and vile and always positioning himself to take advantage of others. A little bit of research made it perfectly clear that Umberto had likely befriended Bernat for the express purpose of taking over the vineyard—as that was what he'd done with the others in the vintners' group Umberto had created to begin his foray into global winemaking.

What he wanted was the Calixto Enterprises business, of course, which Bernat had turned into a multinational wine concern.

At first Pau thought the coincidence of his knowing Giaco was too great to be anything but planned and likely a plot in and of itself, but he soon thought better of that. Umberto merely liked to collect things that made him wealthier and more powerful, and he did not care at all who he hurt in the process. He had perhaps only begun to think about wine thanks to Giaco's friendship with Pau, but there was nothing more sinister there. Umberto hadn't sent his impossible son off to Cambridge as some kind of spy. The very idea was ludicrous.

For one thing, Giaco was ungovernable. He'd never do it. He'd be a shit spy.

That meant Bernat had been collateral damage.

Not long after Pau's discovery, Pau and Giaco had vowed that they would take Umberto down.

Giaco had already gotten his revenge, though it had taken years. Pau had thrown himself into the family business and pulled it back from the brink—and out of Umberto's claws. Umberto, who clearly believed that Pau had no idea what an influence he'd had on Bernat. Or perhaps he simply assumed that no one else cared about the fate of their relatives, as he certainly did not.

Pau had made it seem as if Umberto was finally getting what he wanted from the Calixto family, only to snatch it away from him at the very last moment. Worse, he'd made it clear that he was giving Giaco the very thing Umberto had wanted all this time.

It was satisfying—but it wasn't *personal* enough for Pau.

Bernat might have loved only his vines, but Pau was his son. He'd looked up to his father. He'd wanted, badly, to live up to his father's example.

He knew he would never possess a thread of his father's honor.

So now it was Pau's turn to twist the knife in deeper.

He was quite certain that his friend had no idea how Pau intended to go about claiming his own, private revenge. Pau might even have given Giaco reason to believe that he was as satisfied as Giaco was with the deal they'd pulled off, so that no one would suspect what Pau was up to. The deal they'd engineered left Umberto with significantly less power and money—the only thing the old man cared about—than before.

But Pau had always known that there was one more chess piece to play.

He'd understood full well that there would be consequences for playing it, but that hadn't stopped him.

It wouldn't stop him now.

For here he was with Umberto's pregnant daughter—Giaco's pregnant sister—who had not only slept with Pau but gifted him her innocence. It really was looking a lot like victory.

He tamped down his temper with the strength he'd learned over these long years, and gazed at her.

"Please," he invited Leontina. "Tell me about your father."

She sighed, and looked down at the food without reaching for her plate again. "He's always made it clear that the only utility I offer him is in who he can marry me off to. It's very dynastic. Very dramatically otherworldly, you might even say."

"It is par for the course among men of his wealth and station." Pau shrugged. "After all, everything is a game to them. Why not a child's happiness?"

"I feel certain that my father has never once considered his children's happiness," Leontina said, again with that smile of hers that seemed so charming and yet Pau was certain she was hiding her true feelings somewhere deep beneath it. "In any case, the time has apparently come for me to do my duty. He's chosen a few likely suitors."

Then she named the men in question and Pau felt his whole body seem to...ice over.

One so-called suitor was little better than a warlord. Another was renowned in part for the family company that he had inherited and had not run to ground, but was even better known for his long line of women that he paid to remain quiet after they spent any time with him. The others were more of the same. Very wealthy, very twisted, very revolting men who shared only one thing in common. They had different kinds of power and money.

And Pau knew that Umberto had to be desperate for that. For anything that would elevate him back to the level of power and authority he felt he deserved.

Not that he wouldn't have sold his daughter off anyway, because he had always indicated he would. He was that kind of man. A son was meant to carry his legacy. A daughter was a bargaining chip. But Pau was as certain as he could be that the list of suitors for Umberto Tavian's only daughter would have looked different if it had been drawn up a year ago.

Back before Umberto had been rendered weak and ineffectual by the son he'd always thought was a waste of space.

"I do not see a future of wedded bliss with any of the people you've mentioned," he told Leontina. After a moment.

"Indeed not," she agreed. "Or anything even distantly approaching happiness, for that matter. Not that I require happiness, of course, the world being what it is. But I wouldn't mind the *possibility*, you understand."

She didn't ask him anything directly. He couldn't be sure that she intended not to ask, or if she was simply indicating that there were broader concerns at play. Concerns that she'd decided the father of her baby needed to know before his child was raised as another man's.

Pau then had to sit there and look as if he was mulling things over when the reality was—this was exactly what he'd wanted.

This was his revenge made real.

There was no small part of him that wanted to celebrate this, and loudly.

But it wouldn't do to gloat. Leontina Tavian was not what he'd expected at all—not that night after the wedding and not today—and that was going to take some getting used to. Pau wasn't used to being surprised. He wasn't used to any person, place, or thing defying his expectations. It simply didn't happen.

Or hadn't in a long, long while.

He couldn't tell if it was an act she was putting on as she sat here or if she really was this…extraordinarily unfazed.

It was a question he was going to have to answer, though not right now.

Right now, what he could not do, because it would cause undue chaos in his own life—and Pau did not allow his life to be messy, ever—was to let her know that he'd planned all this from the beginning. He had sought her out, seduced her, and had kept going all night long in the hope of this precise outcome.

He had to sit there for a while. He had to sell it.

He could not let her see that this was a victory, not today. Not yet.

"I suppose it doesn't matter," he said, after some while. Then his gaze found hers and held, and he could not seem to control the intensity in his voice then. "Because if you are carrying the heir to Calixto Enterprises—if you are carrying *my child*—then I fear, Leontina, that the only man you will marry is me."

CHAPTER THREE

It was all excruciatingly civilized.

They agreed that they would marry the next week—that it made the most sense given the situation. They agreed on various timelines to reveal their union and impending parenthood to Umberto, depending on how he responded to Leontina's absence.

"Surely he will send an armed battalion to haul you back into the marriage of his dreams," Pau said in that controlled way of his that Leontina found she was struggling with, because she remembered the fire she'd seen that night all too well—

But she supposed there was time enough to look for it.

"My father will first have to accept that I have actually left," she said. "Then come to what will seem to him the impossible conclusion that I do not intend to return. I imagine he will first cut off my funds, as that is his primary source of control. He will then seethe about for some while, *certain* that I will cave and come crawling back. Only when he begins to believe that I won't be doing that will he send in the cavalry. But he won't have the slightest idea where to look for me, you see. So really we have all the time we need."

Pau only studied her as she delivered this monologue, everything about him *cool* and *unreadable*. "Then I should think it might be best to wait for the child to be born, the better to present him with a family rather than an errant daughter. Far more difficult to brush aside."

As if Pau Calixto himself was a gnat to be waved off.

Leontina put that aside, too. *Eyes on the prize*, she cautioned herself. She needed to be properly and legally married. That was the important thing—and it was a ticking clock.

They agreed that it made sense to sign certain documents, so that each of them maintained what was rightfully theirs no matter what occurred in their marriage. Leontina had no problem with this. Only extremely foolish people gambled away whatever fortune they might have in the hopes that the person they were marrying would live up to whatever ideals they carried in their head.

Leontina had never had much cause to be particularly idealistic.

They even discussed sex.

"That night at your brother's wedding was not my finest hour," Pau told her, sounding apologetic.

Leontina had immediately wanted to murder him for saying that, possibly with her hands, because her memories of that night were all fine. More than fine. "Which hour?" she asked, and smiled sweetly when he lifted a brow. "There were so many hours, as I recall."

"I understand that pregnancy takes a toll on the

body," Pau said, with a great solicitousness that in no way eased the murderous urge inside her. "You will not need to worry about any demands on my part. We can revisit such things after the child is born and we can be assured that all is well and healthy."

What could she do but smile back at him, with that meekness that had never settled into her well? "How kind," she murmured.

Pau gave her a wing of the house to use as her own. And despite the fact that she had grown up in a literal castle, she had significantly more space in Pau's home. He did not have a central library but, instead, there were books in every room. Any place that books could be stacked or shelved, there were more of them than could fit neatly in any of those spaces. Even more intriguing, the books were all clearly well read—even loved. There were cracked spines on old and tattered paperbacks, some of them taped up as if the reader could not bear to part with them.

She knew how books like that looked. She had more than a few of those she'd loved so well herself.

It was quite a difference from her father's showy and impersonal library, clearly installed because people of his wealth and consequence were perceived to be the sort to have libraries, so therefore he needed one. Not because he cared about books, or reading, or the sweet dislocation of looking up from the pages of a book that was so immersive that the reader had forgotten that she was reading at all. She'd been *that deep* in the story.

The books all over this old monastery suggested a very different approach to books and reading. And possibly therefore also life in general, she thought, and

Leontina wanted very much to ask Pau about it. She wanted to understand. Was this a house where people read as a matter of course? Where reading was less a strange pastime that always seemed to provoke comment and was simply…a thing that people did? Like eating or sleeping?

A biological necessity, in other words.

This felt like a revolution inside her, but she did not talk to Pau about such things.

They had talked only of practicalities, not *life philosophies* as related to books.

And the more she thought about his talk of sex—or rather, his talk of no sex despite the night that had brought them here—the more she found herself feeling guilty. Pau was widely renowned to be a man of great virtue, but she had set out to seduce him.

Not only had she succeeded in seducing him, she was now living in his house and planning to marry him. She had known that he would be that kind of stand-up, dependable man. She had been certain that was who he really was, that it wasn't any kind of act.

Now she almost wished it was, because despite the fact that she wouldn't change a thing, she found herself feeling a kind of shame that it had all worked so beautifully.

How was that any different from her father's nasty little plots?

The trouble was that Pau was being nothing but kind and honorable when she knew full well it had been no accident. How could she sit with the knowledge that she'd schemed her way into both her pregnancy and his proposal and then sit him down and discuss…his reading habits and possible bookworm status?

Obviously she couldn't.

That would make her something much closer to a monster, she thought. A bit too Umberto for her tastes when she'd thought that she'd gone to excessive lengths to make certain she was nothing like that man.

Nothing at all… And yet here she was, living what was essentially a lie because it suited her.

She didn't like the comparison.

Leontina drove down into the coastal city of Tarragona one day to do something about the entire lack of a wardrobe she'd brought with her. At first she found herself defaulting to choosing the sorts of clothes she normally wore, but then she stopped herself. Because it occurred to her that maybe—no matter how she'd gotten here—she didn't have to hide any longer.

It was a revolutionary thought.

Maybe this new life she'd snatched out of the dark hole of her previous one was her opportunity to be… whoever the hell she really was. Whoever she'd buried away long before anyone could come along and see the truth of who she actually was inside.

Whoever she might have been if she hadn't had to spend the whole of her life hiding. Usually in plain sight while she pretended she couldn't hear the things that her father and his groupies muttered about her on the rare occasions they noticed her at all.

What if she didn't have to be that Leontina any longer—or ever again?

The real truth was, Leontina wasn't entirely certain that even she knew who she was if left to her own devices. Because she had only ever experimented with it the one time. The one night.

The night she'd dressed with seduction in mind—and she hadn't thrown together a few things and hoped for the best. She had studied Pau Calixto. She had gone to great trouble to find pictures of any woman who had ever been in Pau's vicinity to try to see if there was some common thread she could pull and she'd found it. She'd assembled an outfit that was elegant and form-fitting. She'd kept her makeup subtle. She'd twisted her hair up and had worn her mother's jewelry because it was exquisite without being showy.

And she'd known the moment she'd approached him that she'd gotten it right.

It had been the way he'd looked at her.

Leontina might not have seen that look on anyone's face before—or that heat in a man's eyes as they locked to hers—but she'd understood what it was. She'd *felt* it.

Words had seemed to flow so easily between them. Everything had felt like light, like magic.

Like there were somewhere—anywhere—else than Umberto's castle.

Taking his hand and letting him lead her away from the party had felt as easy as breath. Kissing him had felt like a necessity.

Only now, in a city in Spain she'd never visited before, did she understand that it was only in Pau's arms that she had ever felt that way. Like the truest version of herself.

No hiding. No dissembling.

Just that light, that magic, that seemed to her to last a whole lifetime when it had only been one night.

Maybe, she thought now, that was the truth she needed to claim if she couldn't bring herself to tell him the *whole* truth. And she could start with the clothing she needed to buy. She could dress the way she wanted to dress—not the way that made the most sense because she wanted to be left alone in her father's house.

Though she cautioned herself that she needed to keep it practical. Surely that was the only way to show how grateful she was for how easy Pau had made all of this on her. Because she certainly didn't intend to open up a can of worms and tell him that none of this was his fault, or confess to what she'd done to get them here. So that left only acquiescing to the way he clearly intended to run things between them.

Practical was the name of the game.

And yet somehow, when she got back to the monastery from her shopping excursion, she found that she hadn't bought herself any of her usual shapeless items at all. She hadn't bought anything that was quite as seductive as what she'd worn to her brother's wedding—because that wasn't who she was, either. But the difference was, she was deeply pleased with what she'd chosen. She felt like *herself* even though she knew perfectly well that she wasn't in her normal, blend-in-with-the-furniture attire—maybe that was the point—when she walked down to dinner that night, a ritual that Pau had insisted upon.

After all, he'd said that first afternoon while they'd been so politely hammering out their terms and competing to see who could be more agreeable, more sanguine, which she found herself more and more irritated by the more she thought about it, *we are to be married. We are to be parents. Surely we should know each other a little.*

She was sure she'd seen that banked fire in his gaze then, a reminder of exactly how they found themselves in the situation—but it had been gone again in an instant.

You will not need to worry about any demands on my part, he had told her.

Kindly.

Leontina thought a lot about that, too.

And tonight, as then, it was as if she was looking at a different person altogether when the staff led her to the dining room where Pau waited.

There was more than one dining room in this whimsical house, laid out in increasingly erratic wings that told the story of the centuries it had stood here and the whims of its inhabitants. Some of these dining areas had views. Some were exercises in ostentation. If there was a rhyme or reason to how they were chosen each night, Pau did not share his rationale.

It was one more thing she didn't ask about.

"I see your shopping trip was a success," he said with no particular inflection when she walked in.

And there it was again. The hint of fire in his gaze—

But on the heels of that answering surge of heat inside her, all she could feel in return was that bright surge of guilt that settled on her like a too-warm blanket.

Because unless she was mistaken, and she was rarely mistaken about the people she'd taken the time to study, Leontina was fairly certain that this man was under the impression that he had seduced her that night. That he had somehow taken advantage of her innocence—or why else would he have mentioned her virginity the way he had?

What she'd discovered was that it turned out that it was one thing to plot and scheme in theory. It was another thing to look directly into the face of the man she'd trapped into this situation, whose child she could feel like an insistent weight in her belly, and understand that in this scenario she was nothing but the sort of liar she'd gone to such pains to escape from.

And would remain a liar, she thought as she took her seat and did her best not to pull at the neckline of her dress. It wasn't even particularly revealing, but there was something about the way Pau's cool gaze moved over her flesh. It made her whole body seem to *shimmer*.

Tonight, like every night so far, they sat at a perfectly set table under an umbrella of exquisite politeness.

"How was your day?" she found herself asking, because surely that was the sort of thing a person ought to ask. How would she know? She'd spent most forced meals with her family trying to disappear into her chair.

"Quite pleasant," Pau replied.

He did not elaborate.

They then ate in silence, until it clearly dawned on him that to remain polite, he would have to take a turn at saying something. "You will have to tell me why it is that you chose that particular car for your journey," he said. She looked up at him and found a certain assessing look on his face. "A 1957 Ferrari 335 S Spider Scaglietti. A rare treasure."

When she only gazed back at him in incomprehension, because the car was one of her father's toys—a red convertible like any number of red convertibles her father had scattered around the globe, because apparently he liked a red convertible—Pau's brow lifted.

"I believe only four were ever made." He sounded as if he was displeased—or perhaps it was *disappointed*—that she didn't know this.

"I would love to tell you that there's a story about that car," she told him with an involuntary laugh, because imagine having *stories* about *cars*. "Something I could pretend was casual and yet you could somehow dive beneath the surface and see me for who I really am, perhaps? But alas, I grabbed the first pair of keys I could find and drove here in the car they went with. There was very little choice involved."

"That appears to be a defining feature in your life," Pau said. Mildly.

So very mildly that it took Leontina longer than it should have to understand that he'd struck a blow. She felt the impact of it before she fully comprehended it.

"Are you suggesting that I don't make my own choices in life?" she asked when she understood why it was she felt hollow, suddenly. She blinked, then focused on him. "Do you think that you do?"

That was dangerous, evidently, because suddenly she could feel that danger right there in the room with them. Tonight's dining experience was all about wide-open doors that led out to the patio and looked out over the vineyards. It was beautiful, but she couldn't spare a glance at the reliably stunning landscape.

Not when Pau was eyeing her from across the table, that perfect face of his set into speculative lines and the tension in the room so intense now that she could feel all the fine hairs on her arms stand on end.

"Surely you're joking," he said after a moment, though if he thought so, he certainly didn't indicate that he found her at all amusing. "I feel certain you know who I am, Leontina, and what I have accomplished in this life. No one has ever suggested that I somehow lack the ability to control my own destiny."

That should have been the end of it. She could see that he wanted it to be, that the way his words landed—curt and certain—should have silenced her immediately. But she had been silent a very long time already, hadn't she?

It suddenly seemed to her that if she ceded her voice here, in this new place that promised a new life, than she might as well have stayed behind at the castle and let Umberto do with her what he would.

An unacceptable end, so Leontina waved a hand to the view outside and then took in the old monastery that stood all around them.

"This land controls you as surely as my father controls me," she told him matter-of-factly. "It's the Calixto family legacy and it controls your destiny no matter what choices you do or do not make. It is no different for me, though I do not get the opportunity to preen about in boardrooms talking in secret corporate code words that make other men think I'm a profound genius in all I do."

Pau seemed to…*expand*, though she could see with her own eyes that he did not actually move. He stayed where he was, sitting in his seat across the table from her, those long, blunt-edged fingers of his tapping against the stem of his wineglass.

"That's quite an indictment, Leontina. And I can only assume you're speaking of your father when you speak of preening." His expression shifted slightly. "Or perhaps your brother. What I know is that you cannot possibly think you are describing *me*."

No one had offered her wine, which she knew was in deference to her pregnancy, but Leontina found it somehow emblematic of this entire experience. She was sitting on the grounds of one of the most famous and widely celebrated vineyards in the world. With a glass of sparkling water.

Those were the choices that *she* made.

"I was never given the opportunity to express myself or my feelings about my family legacy through universities or boardrooms," she told him, and was proud of how even her voice sounded when she felt so ragged inside. "What's expected of me is my obedience. But I'll be honest with you. I don't see a whole lot of difference between your situation and mine."

He didn't speak. She wasn't sure he moved, and yet she was certain she could see his resistance to that notion as if it was written all over him.

In bold print.

She kept going. "Here we both are, about to marry a near-stranger almost entirely because our legacies demand it. No shirking of responsibilities for us. I might be running from less pleasant options, I grant you. But the only thing that's changed in my life is that, three months ago, I did in fact make a choice." She lifted her shoulder and then dropped it. "I suppose we could say that really, I'm the only one who made any choices here."

And until she saw a flash of something that looked a good deal like temper move over his beautiful face, she didn't realize that this was what she wanted from him. She *wanted* to see behind his cool, closed-down exterior. Because she was starting to think that all those images she still had in her head of what had happened between them that night were a dream.

If she couldn't feel the baby she carried inside her, Leontina would be certain she'd imagined the whole thing.

She held her breath, thinking that he would explode at her temerity, and wondering why she was dancing so close to telling him truths she knew full well she should keep to herself—

But instead, he merely inclined his head. He took a sip of his wine.

And it was as if nothing had happened. As if there had been no intensity, no flash of anything, no wild sensation all over that had made her skin prickle.

As if she'd imagined all that, too.

They carried on in exactly the same *careful* way until the day of their wedding one week after her arrival in Spain, where, if possible, everything became even *more* stiff and formal.

It was a swift and unemotional ceremony on one of the many terraces with sweeping views of the vine-covered land. The weather was bright and blue, but not too hot, as if the sun knew better than to get too carried away over such a matter-of-fact ceremony. The priest had clearly been briefed, because he kept his comments to a minimum. They exchanged their vows quietly and without fuss. Pau had produced rings before the ceremony and they both placed the appropriate one on each other's appropriate hand.

Really, it was like they were acting out a wedding instead of participating in one, Leontina thought.

Until, when bid by the priest, they pressed their lips together.

That did not feel at all like acting.

She felt a kind of shock race through her at the brush of his warm mouth against hers but it was so fleeting and gone so quickly that she wasn't sure she hadn't imagined that, either.

Even though she could remember kissing him the moment they'd moved indoors and were alone in her father's castle—the way she had moved closer to him and dared to kiss him right there in the hall, the way his mouth had opened on hers with all of that immediate, fiery heat, the way he had wrapped his arms around her and ate at her mouth as if he was starving for the taste—

Leontina had to remind herself that he had decreed there would be no *demands*.

Even if, that night, there had been nothing but demands. And the meeting of those demands.

Again and again and again.

After the wedding concluded with none of the fanfare normally associated with such a moment, she and Pau stayed behind once the priest and the two witnesses—both staff that Leontina suspected that he had chosen for their unreadably wooden expressions—took their leave.

When he made no move to follow them, she thought

perhaps one of them would say a few words. Or ought to, anyway, though she found her throat strangely dry.

Not to mention the flush she was sporting because she was reliving their night together in her head, to no avail.

Pau stared out at the vines. Always the vines. Leontina thought she saw a muscle working in the hinge of his jaw. But when he looked at her, his gaze was cool. "Our child will now be legitimate. And you need not worry about your father's dynastic aspirations any longer. I believe we have handled the situation with grace, Leontina."

"The very picture of grace," she managed to say, though it felt inadequate.

And largely untrue, given all the things they'd done that first night at the castle to make all of this happen. Though this was still not the time to start thinking about all that, she cautioned herself when her brain took the opportunity to flood her with images from the bed they'd shared. And the chair. And the rug before the fireplace. And the shower. And the bath—

She reached down, subtly she hoped, and pinched her own side. Hard. Until the images faded. Because if *he* could pretend there wasn't all that wild heat swimming about between them, so could she.

Leontina thought he might say something else since he was still standing there before her, that muscle working in his jaw. But instead he inclined his head in that way of his that she was coming to hate, turned with something like military precision, and left her there as he marched into the house.

For a long while, she simply…stayed there. Right where she was.

Right where he'd left her.

Leontina stood at the rail, staring straight ahead, taking in the sweep of the earth before her. The imposing, copper-hued Montsant Mountains that rose in the distance. The rugged land itself, cultivated now but in no way free of its wildness.

It was a beautiful afternoon. She could hear birds singing. The buzz of lazy insects. The air smelled of sage, rosemary, and oregano. There were leafy green trees she was fairly certain were hazelnut. The sun danced over everything, making it gleam like the diamond she now wore on her hand.

She was pregnant, married, and—once again—entirely alone.

Leontina did not realize until that very moment that she had expected that things would be different, now. She hadn't understood that she was holding on to that possibility until this moment, when it was so obviously unattainable. She hadn't understood that deep inside her, she'd been holding out a secret little spark of hope that coming to Spain, tracking down Pau, and successfully marrying someone who she was reasonably certain was in no way a monster like the rest of her father's questionable choices of potential spouses would lead somewhere.

That all the things she'd felt that long, hot night might mean something.

All those impossible things that felt like magic in the moment but had taken on different hues later. When she'd missed her first period. When she'd started to imagine her baby and the man who'd fathered it.

She'd begun to wonder if those moments of connection were more than the heat of it all. That they truly meant that she might have set out to seduce the one person alive who could actually make her feel *alive*.

Herself, at last.

A whole woman who could laugh and love and be praised for these things instead of made to feel like something was terribly wrong with her.

She'd imagined that it was possible that Pau Calixto was not merely her escape plan, but her fate.

Or at least, when she was feeling more *practical*, she'd imagined that it all *could* mean something. She could admit, now, *today*, that she'd hoped it could. Or lead somewhere once she made it here.

Or maybe, she thought now, a little more bitterly than she liked, *just end up with me less alone for once.*

But even as she thought that, her hands snuck down and found their way over the swell of her belly. She had only really just started to show. It was still something she could conceal, if she liked. In the dress she'd chosen today, a pale blue because she hadn't felt that the full on bridal approach was warranted, she doubted anyone could see a bump at all.

Yet she knew it was there.

She knew her baby was *right there*.

Meaning she was literally *not* alone, no matter how she might feel. There was another human inside her, and something about that seemed to wash over her like the breeze on her face. Like the priest's blessing.

Like the wishes she'd never dared make out loud, but had somehow held tight inside her all along.

Maybe that was why, later that evening, she did not wait for a formal summons to another meticulously polite dinner with the man who was now her husband and some days—like today, their wedding day—might as well be a robot. Still dressed in her wedding attire, she went in search of him instead.

Leontina wandered through the old, sprawling monastery, wondering how many old fingerprints were hidden behind the polished walls, the modernized rooms. How many ghosts were here with her, watching her as she walked down one long hall and into another.

She didn't know the house well, but it was laid out flat, so it was easy enough to follow one hallway to its end, retrace her steps, and then go down another one until she found herself in a whole wing of the house she'd never seen before.

But she knew immediately that it was his.

Leontina fancied that she caught that scent of his as she walked down the hall, hints of vetiver and cedar clinging to the very walls the way she'd thought they'd clung to her for days after the wedding. And all the way down at the end of the hallway, though she glimpsed other rooms as she passed—sitting rooms, parlors, entertainment caves, and all of them stuffed full with even more books—she found him in an office that had its own door to the outside and a stairway that led down to what she knew were the vineyard's commercial offices. Leontina was certain that she made no noise, but he turned anyway, making her wonder if he was as aware of her she was of him.

But then, she'd known that he was the night of her brother's wedding. She'd known the moment she walked out into the reception that he was watching her.

She'd felt his eyes on her as she moved.

It had felt like they were in a dance from the start.

And when he turned now, he wasn't prepared for her. She could see the difference at once. Because when his eyes met hers, they widened—

Like that, she understood at last.

This was all a mask. That volcanic lover who'd turned her inside out and taught her things about herself that she wasn't entirely certain she wished to know—

The man who had shown her how sensual her body was, and all the things that she could do with it—

He was *right here*.

He had been here all along.

It was that wildfire flash, lighting up that dark gaze of his, and then gone when he collected himself.

But what it told Leontina, with the same certainty she'd felt out on that terrace earlier, was that she wasn't alone in her marriage, either.

No matter what he might pretend.

And so when Pau frowned at her while he crossed the room toward her, she didn't smile. She didn't try to make this easy and polite and *practical* again.

"Is something the matter?" he asked, in that distant, cool, vaguely *quizzical* voice of his.

Leontina decided that she really did hate it. "That's a loaded question on this of all days. Surely even you can see that."

He let that quizzical expression on his face shift into something that was somehow colder, more resigned—

and yet indicated that she was not making any sense. And she hated that, too.

That was the kind of expression that had led to all those stilted dinners, and she was done with them. God, she needed to be *done* with things that made her feel like she was stuck under her father's thumb.

She needed to feel anything—everything—but alone.

And so when he drew even closer, scanning her as if he expected to find her with some sort of head wound to justify her appearance in this sacred temple of corporate glory—his office—she stopped waiting. She stopped wondering if he was going to do something to shift the balance between them.

Instead, Leontina swayed forward, as if she was perhaps losing her balance.

When he moved to take her arm, she flowed toward him. Closer in, he smelled as marvelous as she recalled—better. She went up on her toes, slid a hand up to cup the nape of his neck, and kissed him.

Not the way she'd kissed him outside today, chaste and infuriating.

Leontina kissed him the way she'd wanted to kiss him for three months.

Deep and hot and filled with all the wildness and wonder he'd taught her himself.

CHAPTER FOUR

It was like a great dam broke inside Pau, and once it did, there was no reclaiming higher ground. It was swept away in an instant and he knew immediately that there was no hope of getting it back.

He might as well surrender to the flood. It was that or be lost in it himself.

And he had done his best at the wedding ceremony. He had kissed her as the ceremony required, but he'd made sure that it was barely a kiss at all. A dry peck, nothing more, even though every part of him had been seized with the urge to get his hands on her for real. And taste her again, at last.

The way he'd dreamed all these months.

Now she'd undone all his good work. His sacrifice. His self-control.

Because now that her mouth was on his, he was done for—no matter what he tried to tell himself.

He hadn't expected that the tool of his revenge would taste like this, was the thing. All that heat and glory. That punch deep in his gut. Nothing in his life had readied himself for something like Leontina. He hadn't thought to prepare himself for such an onslaught of passion that it had nearly knocked him over in Italy.

It was the same here, in his family's ancestral home.

It was—and he could no longer pretend otherwise—simply Leontina. This was what she did to him. This was who she made him.

Pau had never been much like Giaco, with his big appetite for all forms of intimacies—made even more voracious in service to their plans for Umberto, to build the perfect picture they'd known the old man would use to dismiss his son entirely. Pau had applauded Giaco's efforts—and energy—but Pau himself had always preferred intensity to volume.

Leontina's kiss proved, yet again, that he'd never really experienced intensity at all.

Not before her.

But it also proved that he hadn't been making things up to suit his narrative three months ago. This woman simply set him on fire, and the part of that he found the most maddening was that he didn't think she was trying.

It was simply *her*. It was Leontina herself. It was this impossible chemistry that raged between them no matter what he told himself.

And Pau had never been the kind of man who interrupted an afternoon's work for the pleasures of the flesh, or any pleasures whatever—

But he couldn't seem to keep his arms from wrapping themselves around her body. He couldn't seem to prevent himself from lifting her up off the floor and holding her high against his chest as he devoured her in turn.

And then, somehow, he was sliding his hands down the soft curve of her spine so that he could grip her fine, surprisingly lush bottom.

He held her tight, pressed there against his cock, so hard and ready for her it bordered on pain.

Pau kissed her and kissed her, unable to tell where he ended and she began because it was all the same impossible sensation. And he remembered it too well from before.

It had blown up just like this. He'd been similarly knocked flat by the sheer *heat* of it. Of her mouth on his. Of the slightest touch of her hand.

They had talked at the reception, and she had been the one to touch him first. She had been the one to angle herself closer to him. When he had suggested they take a stroll, she had smiled with too much light in her eyes and he had wondered—for the first time in his life—if he had what it took to keep his hands off her until they were alone.

The answer to that was no, he didn't have anything remotely resembling his usual fierce sense of honor and comportment, because she'd looked up at him with a ferocity that had made him shiver and his cock rock hard, and had kissed him like her life depended on it.

Pau had found himself wondering if, in fact, his did.

He'd kissed her back wildly, heedlessly. Recklessly.

And it had all gotten worse from there.

The truth was that he could have had sex with her once, that night. It would likely have been sufficient. But once had been nothing like enough.

Pau had told himself that he was hedging his bets,

but today it was all a lot more clear, whether he liked it or not.

He hadn't been able to let her go.

Not until the sun rose and she snuck away before the light grew too bright, murmuring something about not wanting anyone to know what had happened between them. That had left him to lie there in that ostentatious suite Umberto had given him with fawning fake obsequiousness, knowing that he should be plotting out his next move when instead all he could do was attempt to recover.

He hadn't been prepared for the explosion that was Leontina Tavian.

Here, now, it all made sense. Or anyway, he could use it. He could work with it. She was already his wife. She was pregnant with his child, and showing.

His revenge was already in hand.

And Pau could see no good reason why he shouldn't indulge himself the way he'd wanted to do all along.

Since the moment she'd turned up at his door—and long before that, though he'd waited out the first three months of what he hoped was a potential pregnancy to give the situation time to develop. Only a few weeks ago he'd been studying the calendar, thinking of ways he would find her again. Thinking of how he would renew their connection without the convenience of her brother's wedding, and if she wasn't already pregnant, rectify that at once.

He'd assured himself that he was thinking only of revenge, but he was pleased she'd come to him instead.

And not only—he could admit in this moment—because it made his revenge easier.

Pau set her down on her feet to peel her dress up and over her head, then he tossed it aside. Soon after, he found himself down on his knees before her because it was a physical need. He had to trace the changes in her beautiful body.

Her breasts were rounder now, heavier, and filled his palms. Her waist still nipped in, but there was a noticeable swell in her lower abdomen and he felt his breath shudder out before he pressed his mouth there, too.

A different sort of kiss, perhaps. But it shook through him like a new fire all its own.

His child was right there, beneath his hands. No longer an abstract idea he could wield against Umberto, but soon enough to be a *person*. A complicated human all its own.

Somehow he had never stopped to wonder about this part. About how knowing this woman was pregnant, and knowing exactly how she'd become pregnant, would settle in him and *simmer*.

That she'd married him today only made it better.

He smoothed his hands over her soft skin, her round belly, only aware in the abstract that he was murmuring things. He couldn't even have said what. Spanish. Italian. Bits of French and English. All the languages he knew tangled together as if he couldn't choose just one to honor this moment.

His wife. The mother of his child.

His heart beat on that for some time.

Until he had to remind himself that revenge was the point of this. It had always been the point of this.

But it was hard to care about that when she was

standing there looking down at him, her dark hair twisted back on her head and her dark jade eyes bright

He pulled her down with him, controlling her descent, and then they were tangled on the floor and she was as he remembered her. Leontina was *alight*. She seemed wilder this time. More demanding. Pau wondered if she, too, had dreamed too many vivid dreams these past few months.

They rolled and she straddled him. Then her hands were on the casual shirt he wore, pulling it up and over his head and making a low noise of approval that he felt resonate inside him. Everywhere.

Leontina leaned down and he could feel the heat of her mouth, the sharp sweetness of her tongue, as she traced a shimmering trail of sensation over his bare skin.

They rolled again and he found himself cradled between her thighs. It made him sigh with the pleasure of it. He reached down between them, sliding his hand beneath the panties she wore and stroking his way until he could feel all of her glowing, beautiful heat.

But it wasn't enough to simply hold all that glory in his palm. Pau found himself tracing circles around the center of her need, then plunging one finger deep inside her. Then another. Then, as she hummed and moaned, setting up a slick rhythm because she was molten hot and ready for him.

And he kept going until she convulsed in his arms and came all over him, gasping out his name.

Pau didn't bother undressing, he only reached down and shoved his pants out of the way. And then he simply pulled her panties to the side so he could slam his way deep inside her.

Leontina shattered again, at once, but he didn't give her the space to ride it out. He began to thrust, carrying her as she fell and then building her up again. And as she sobbed and clung to him, as he plunged deep inside her as if they'd been together like this every night since they'd met, he thought of absolutely nothing but the *feel* of this.

Of her.

Her velvet, his steel. The way she clenched tight around him and drew him into her so that together, they could chase that fire that had burned from the start into a wild incandescence.

When she clutched him tight and sobbed out his name once more, her body beginning to clutch around him, he went with her.

And this was how Pau Calixto, who had made his reputation on the correctness of his behavior and his abiding moral rectitude—a deep contrast with many of the other individuals in his tax bracket—came back to himself on the floor of his office, still lodged deep inside Leontina Tavian.

An office that was made almost entirely of windows, into which any member of his staff could have looked at any point. If it had been any time in the last half hour, he wouldn't have cared if they all gathered round and pulled up chairs.

Pau really couldn't tell if he was horrified or something more like…*proud.*

He shoved that word away. It didn't make sense, not here. Not when the entire point of his existence was to live up to his father's exacting expectations. To do it even better than his father had done, and thereby somehow make good on this thing his father had loved. To preserve both the legacy his father had nearly lost and Pau's own along with it.

A legacy that would then carry over to the child she carried, even now.

A chain that bound them all together, holding them tight, throughout generations—something far better, and far more real, than the emotional ties he knew some families spoke of. He believed the Calixto way was better.

Laudable even, he thought, but that didn't change the fact that they were potentially on display.

He stood and put his clothing to rights, then wordlessly helped Leontina back into her dress. Then he put physical distance between them as quickly as he could.

"That can obviously not happen again," he said, the chill in his voice frigid even to his own ears. "This is a business, not a brothel."

Leontina only gazed back at him, her green eyes entirely too calm. "I hate to be that person, but a brothel *is* a business."

"It is not *my* business," he returned. He found himself sliding a hand over his hair and stopped himself, because Pau Calixto did not *fidget*. "I see no need for us to dine together tonight. I will have the staff deliver a tray to your rooms. I appreciate that we were wed today and perhaps emotions were running high, but I thought I made this clear."

Now she looked…interested. Maybe. As if this was

a lecturer she'd caught at university, quite by accident, and she thought she might pull up a chair and listen in.

Then that was literally what she did. She moved over to his desk and settled herself in one of the chairs in front of it, and he despised the fact that she looked perfectly put together when he was contending with a heretofore unknown *fidgeting* problem. Her dark hair didn't look the slightest bit out of place and if he hadn't known exactly where that glow she wore came from, he might have tried to convince himself that it was simply cosmetics at play. Her dress was wholly unwrinkled despite what they'd just done. The ring he'd slid on her finger with his own hands earlier caught the light.

Pau found himself wishing that she was still concealing herself in her baggy sackcloth missing only the attendant ashes, but he hadn't seen the faintest hint of the dress she arrived in. Not in days.

"Please be clear again," she encouraged him, with that damned smile of hers that he knew meant she was *handling* him. "I would hate to accidentally misinterpret anything that happened between us."

Like, for instance, a disgraceful display of animalistic urges on the floor of his office. He could see that she was thinking that, though she didn't say it. She didn't have to say it.

Pau was fairly certain that there was only one way to interpret what had happened between them today, but he didn't want any part of that. He wanted her pregnant. He wanted her married, and to him. He wanted to shove all of that at Umberto, make it hurt, and watch as the vile old man took it in.

He'd always thought that this would be best achieved

with Leontina clearly married to him and a whole child that could not be ignored between them.

The perfect family despite Umberto's vicious little games.

He'd been planning it all out for years. But in all of that planning, he had never considered that he might have his own, unpleasantly emotional reaction to all of those things. It had never occurred to him to solve for that in advance, because never in his life had his cock had a mind of its own.

Pau could not in good conscience allow it to drive his behavior now.

He frowned at Leontina, sitting there so prettily across the desk from him. Still looking as if this was an academic exercise when, as far as he knew, she had never seen the inside of a university classroom. Or possibly any classroom at all, now that he thought about it.

Umberto had not seemed to notice that she existed until she came of age, as her brother always told it.

But he shoved that ugliness aside. "That night at your brother's wedding was a mistake, as I think we can both agree."

He waited for her to murmur her agreement at that, on cue, the way everyone else did when he gave them such openings. But Leontina didn't make a sound. She only gazed back at him, and waited.

Pau couldn't say he cared for that, either. It made him wonder if she could tell that he was lying. That he did not view that night as a mistake at all. But how could she?

He pushed on. "We were both careless, though I blame myself."

"It would be rather silly to blame the virgin, wouldn't it?" she asked, and he thought her voice was just a little *too* dry. But he didn't pursue it.

"Now we have done the decent thing," he continued, nodding as he spoke. "We have executed our duty in the time-honored fashion. We have married. The child will have a name."

"In fairness, the child would have a name either way," Leontina said. Musingly, he was almost sure, except he rather thought there was something a bit *harder* behind the easy tone she used. "It's not as if, were I to give birth on my own, I would somehow overlook the naming part and force the poor child to stumble about namelessly, is it?"

"That is not what I meant."

"I know what you meant." Again, that beatific smile that he was truly beginning to loathe. "It's only that I find these agreements we make so fascinating, don't you? A child has no name unless its father claims him. That claiming legitimizes the child's birth, when surely, being alive is all the legitimacy a child needs. Do you ever wonder why it is we all agree to these things without ever actually discussing them?"

"Money," Pau shot back curtly. "Property. Land and legacy. But I think you know that too, Leontina."

"In any case," she said smoothly, smile in place, "our fully legitimate child is on the way. Congratulations to you, Dad."

He expected to feel horror at that, but horror was not at all the sensation that moved through him. Pau realized that, once again, he was somehow unprepared for this moment. He, who had never been unprepared for anything.

But it kept happening.

With her it seemed to happen with alarming regularity.

He had certainly not been ready for her to kiss him like that, on that first night or today. It was as if he had no defenses against her—and now this. Pau had thought of little else but her pregnancy and their marriage, and her belly beneath his hands had been a revelation, but her calling him *Dad*—even though he knew she was doing it to be provocative—seemed to unlock something inside him.

Something he also hadn't looked at yet, when he was the sort of man who looked at everything from every angle at least a thousand times by rote.

Yet not this astonishing truth: He was going to be a father.

And whatever revenge he could enact upon Umberto Tavian because of that, and would, the fact remained. Pau himself would be a father to a child. He would be responsible for shaping the child, just as his father had shaped him.

It felt…sacred. Overwhelming. *Beautiful.*

He had to look away and he could not account for the tightness in his throat. His chest. He was tempted to imagine he was ill when he never succumbed to the illnesses that plagued others.

"I would appreciate it if you joined me in pretending that this scene today did not happen," he said stiffly. "We'll get along quite well if we keep to our own places and the timelines we've already agreed upon. I have no idea what it is you do all day, but I do not wish to be disturbed when I am working."

"Books," she said.

Opaquely.

When he only stared at her, Leontina smiled—but it was a different smile this time. He felt it like a blow straight through his chest, because he recognized it. He'd seen it before, but only when they were both naked, tangled up together in his bed at the castle.

He could even remember what they had been talking about. She had been telling him the story of how she'd managed to foil her father's plans for her this far into her twenties, when Umberto had made it clear that if it were up to him, he would have sold her off on her eighteenth birthday and been done with it.

Her invisibility powers, such as they were, had involved servants' quarters and a certain blank expression that she'd pulled out to show him, somehow transforming her lovely face into something dull and easily ignored.

Then she'd smiled, just like this.

"I beg your pardon?" He said it stiffly because that damned smile, filled with *joy* of all things, was having the same effect on him now that it had then.

A catastrophic effect, to his mind, because it tempted him to forget himself completely.

"I read books," she told him, gently, as if she didn't expect him to follow. "I realize that's not a career, but that's what I do. My father couldn't be bothered to send me off to university and he'd long since grown bored of my tutors well before I turned sixteen. So I decided to educate myself. I feel it's something of a lifelong pursuit."

"Yes. Well." He found himself clearing his throat. "We have no shortage of books here."

He was sure he saw her gaze get more intent. "Are they all yours?"

"Mine, yes." Now his chest felt even tighter. "Many were my father's, though he preferred more nonfiction than I do, I believe. Even my grandfather was a reader, which is surprising because otherwise, he preferred life's more active indulgences. Gambling. Pretty woman. A private island or two in warm climates where he could relax with said women who, it must be said, flocked to him. They mourned en masse at his funeral."

The papers had talked of it for ages, all those beautiful women in black, mourning a man who had been faithful to none of them—and under the eye of his long-suffering widow, who had famously acted as if she didn't see a single one of them. Bernat had always been deeply scathing about his father. *Not much of a husband or father*, he'd always said. *It's a wonder he didn't burn the whole estate down, the way he carried on.*

Pau could only imagine how apoplectic his father would have been if the estate had been at risk. The true measure of a Calixto man, he'd always believed. It was one more reason for Pau to hate Umberto. Pau might not have thought that his father was a particularly dab hand at parenting, but that wasn't the point of the family. The point of *this* family was the wine and the history.

Umberto had stolen that from Bernat. And Pau could

not bear the knowledge that his father had died thinking he had failed.

He could not *bear* it.

"I'll start reading my way through your house, then," Leontina was saying. "And I also do not wish to be disturbed when I'm deep in a book. But you do know what they say, don't you?"

"I have never given the slightest bit of weight to what *they* say," he retorted, perhaps more harshly than necessary. He tried to claw his way back to calmness as he continued. "I don't even know who *they* are."

"In this case, they are me." Leontina laughed, and that laughter moved all over him, like light. As if she knew the dark place he'd gone and could bring him back that easily. "But I do truly believe that you can really find the bones of a house, or a person I suppose, if you know what they read. So if you'll excuse me, I'll start digging up your family graves, Pau. Who knows what we might find?"

She smiled broadly, but he found that unsettling—and not only because he knew what was buried here, and why. Nothing he needed dug up. Nothing he wanted to haul out into the bright sunshine.

Nothing she needed to worry about until the child was here and it was finally time to make certain his revenge hit the way he'd planned it would. And Pau did not allow himself to wonder how she would react to that, because it didn't matter. It couldn't.

He found everything that had happened there in his office more than merely *unsettling*, if he was honest, because he had the unpleasant notion that it did, in fact, matter to him what Leontina would think. What she would *do*. It kept him awake that night, or perhaps it was his unruly cock and all those images in his head that he'd seen fit to add to today.

Either way, she haunted him.

And he intended to officiously turn her away if she tried to find him again in the days that followed, but of course, she didn't.

Pau was the one who found himself wandering like a ghost in his own house, peering into rooms until he found her. When he did, it was as she'd said. She was always surrounded by books. Always frowning slightly, sometimes playing with her lower lip, completely lost in the pages that she turned.

He had not realized that when she said that she read books, what she'd meant was that she *inhaled* them. *Consumed* them.

Became them.

He told himself that he was not the least bit jealous of the attention she lavished upon inanimate objects. But he did insist that the staff usher her to dinner a week or so later, choosing a different room to dine in the way he always did, because they had never had family dinners when he was a child and he was determined to find the *best* one before the child arrived.

Tonight he was as close to agitated as he allowed himself to get, for he'd barely seen her except in those stolen ghost glances, when she hadn't even known he was there.

Speaking of things he had not thought to plan or expect, because Leontina was forever a wildcard.

"I do hope you can control yourself," he found himself saying, stuffy and frigid, when she entered the room.

He hadn't seen her up close in a while. He'd been driving himself crazy remembering the taste of her. That sea-salt-and-honey scent that was only hers, and made him hard even to recall. The sounds she made. The way the heat of her held him, clutched in tight.

Maybe that was what made him unduly ferocious tonight—but all she did was laugh.

Leontina laughed, and then she reached over and patted him on his jaw as if he was a child.

"Don't worry," she said. Soothingly. "I am also quite hungry tonight. For food."

And as she swept past him, settling herself at the table and digging into the platters of food that waited for them, Pau didn't follow.

Because a different truth was dawning upon him.

He found himself turning, slowly, and gazing upon her. Upon this woman who, now that he considered it, wasn't behaving at all the way he would have expected her to.

Pau had spent the last ten days wondering what was happening to him. Was she a witch, to get beneath his defenses like that? What *was* all of this?

But tonight it was as if all the oddities in her reactions to him snapped together, finally forming a full picture. Because it finally occurred to him that he'd been operating under the mistaken impression that her physical innocence meant she was innocent in all other ways too—when this did not track.

She had told him as much, had she not? She had shown him her disguise—and the fact that she was here with him in Spain meant that she'd handily foiled her father's plans for her, when that was something that had taken him and Giaco years upon years to accomplish.

Now, at last, Pau remembered the way she'd been dressed at that wedding. A complete departure from the way she'd dressed in the days before to scuttle unnoticed about the castle—and he'd been watching her. It had been night and day, in fact. *So* night and day that it had to have been planned.

Meticulously planned, he thought now, because it wasn't as if she'd been tottering around, looking awkward and uncomfortable, the way women sometimes did when they decided to try on a new look but didn't know if it suited them.

Leontina, quite obviously, knew exactly what suited her.

She'd been a dream come true, all sex and elegance.

It wasn't only that. Now that he considered it, she hadn't spoken to anyone else at that wedding, aside from the briefest interaction with her father and a few words with her brother and new sister-in-law after the ceremony.

A lot like she'd been focused on Pau—and only Pau—all along.

He had to sit with that, because it had literally never occurred to Pau that it was remotely possible that his best friend's younger sister, famously sheltered and hidden away in an actual castle with a drawbridge, could possibly have her own agenda.

And had enacted this agenda. Was enacting it now, he rather thought.

Pau found himself walking over to the dinner table in something of a daze. He took his seat and found his wineglass, though a taste of his family's finest vintage did nothing to clear his head.

She had been innocent. He had known that going in, but in the moment it had taken precious little to convince her to come along with him. He had felt the wildfire chemistry between them too and had chalked it all up to that unexpected connection, but it had all been…smooth. Especially once she kissed him and set it all in motion. And he had been so focused on the end result that it hadn't occurred to him to question what *she* was doing.

But now he saw her. He truly saw all of her.

Pau thought about how she had taken charge in his office, kissing him in a way she had to have known would lead exactly where it had led.

He thought about how the same thing had happened at her father's castle. Leontina had been the one to sway closer to him as it got dark. She had been the one to put her hand on his arm and she had also been the one to press her lips against his.

And he'd taken it from there—but Pau had always been good at probabilities. He wasn't certain how he'd missed them so completely this time.

But he could calculate them swiftly as he took in his wife's happy expression as she ate. Bordering on *content*, even, in circumstances that should have been a bit more delicate, surely. A bit harder to come to terms with.

Pau understood at last that she'd been playing him all along. That she'd walked into that wedding reception with every intention of making happen what had, indeed, happened. Over and over and over again that night.

And that meant a great number of things, all of which he would need to sort through.

But tonight, he could only focus on the most important of those things.

She had been playing him this entire time while he'd actually felt some measure of shame that he'd seduced her the way he had. He'd had his reasons for doing it, but he'd still felt bad about the whole thing.

Once again, he thought about that memory that had surfaced earlier, of her showing him how she could hide in plain sight. How she could hide *herself* so that people could look at her and see right through her.

How she had shown him exactly how she did it.

And yet he had never put those things together. Until tonight.

Now he finally realized that she'd been seducing him in turn. That it had all gone swimmingly because they were *both* seducing *each other*.

The only difference now was that she didn't know that he'd figured her out.

He sat with that all through dinner.

"You let me know when you're finished being brooding and silent," she said to him, soothingly, when dinner was finished. She had one hand on her belly and he thought she did that unconsciously now. Holding on to the child as she got up from her seat and stood there. He liked that more than he should have.

But he said nothing in reply, and that made her laugh again.

Not, he thought, the way an innocent caught up in a

game she hadn't understood she was playing would act. If he was certain of nothing else, he was certain of that.

"Very well, then," she said. "I'll go back to tracking down clues about you in all the books you left with weathered pages and broken spines. I wonder which one of us will know the other one better when I'm done, Pau."

Something in him roared at that, though he couldn't tell if it was a warning or simply a reaction. Not that it mattered.

He listened to her footsteps as she walked away, back down the hallway, and likely back to a stack of books to lose herself in. He didn't call her out. He didn't tell her he knew what she'd been doing.

Instead, he thought, why not keep playing the role he'd already been castigating himself about?

Pau could act like the dark seducer he thought he'd been for her. It wasn't any kind of hardship. Staying away from her was the hard part—and why should he bother? He had only been doing it as he felt he owed it to her, as some kind of apology for having seduced her into this mess.

But he hadn't, had he?

He took another pull from his wine, and started calculating the best line of attack.

Because an attack it was, and Pau had always been excellent at building an offensive.

And maybe, while he was at it, he'd fuck the truth right out of her at last.

CHAPTER FIVE

As COLD, DISTANT, and relentlessly practical as their first week together had been, that was how outrageously, dangerously hot it all became as the season mellowed deeper into a vibrant fall.

Because Pau had shifted everything after that scene in his office. He'd swept her up into his arms and carried her to his bedroom, where there was no sign of *practicalities* or coolness of any kind.

It was almost as if he'd decided to make every night like that first night, to see if he could literally take her apart that way—

But she told herself she was being dramatic. It was just that he'd finally accepted the wildfire chemistry between them, that was all. If she found him ferocious in his need, brimming with an intensity that would have been too much if she didn't want him with the same deep fervor—well.

She told herself that it only proved that she'd been right all along. There was *something* between them after all. There was this fire that only seemed to burn brighter and hotter every night.

That was enough, she assured herself. It was more than she'd ever had before. It had to be enough.

It was harvest time and Calixto Estates was very busy. The vineyards were always buzzing and the house itself was never as quiet as it had been the week leading up to their wedding. Sometimes Leontina wondered what might have happened if she'd simply waited and let events unfold as they would. Would all of this activity have swept her up in it anyway? Would she have felt differently about things if she'd seen Pau in action, pitching in to help with his own two hands? Would she have learned to think of the land first, the way he did?

Because she was fairly certain that he could have left those things to the hired hands and seasonal workers who worked the harvest every year, but he didn't. He liked to be out there in the middle of everything. She thought, after growing up with Umberto, who never dirtied his own hands with anything, she would have found this impressive.

She would have felt even guiltier about tricking such a good man into marriage.

But Leontina would never know for sure because, once again, she hadn't waited to see what would happen after their wedding ceremony. She hadn't kept a respectful distance the way Pau had intended that they would. She'd jumped in and made things happen, which she would have said was not her personality at all—

Except it appeared that it cwas. Where he was concerned, anyway.

And yet she was just as happy that things had gone the way they were supposed to, she thought one morning as she woke in her usual state of dazed, dark pleasure in Pau's bed.

She stretched and confirmed that he had already left the bed and the room, which was typical. The man never seemed to sleep much. And Leontina knew this because he kept her up half the night, every night. Because there seemed to be no limit to the ways they could explore all the different shades and temperatures of the wildfire that only seemed to blaze hotter between them the more they indulged it.

Most mornings she felt seared through, head to toe and back again.

Because once the man decided to do something, apparently—he did it full on.

This particular morning, she found her hands on her belly as she murmured her usual greetings to the child she carried. She was aware that her bump seemed bigger now. Just as she was aware that for all her talk of choices, the only ones that truly mattered now were the ones she made for and about this child.

Even if it didn't seem that way in the middle of the night when all she could seem to do was sob out Pau's name and beg him for more.

She sat up in his bed and basked in the light that beamed in from the bank of windows set into the old stone walls. Everything was rendered golden like honey, and she felt as if she was bathed in it as she padded over to those windows and looked down, her gaze moving over the usual bustle of activity below. When she found Pau there, right in the thick of things, she felt that familiar pang go through her once again.

It was becoming a part of her now, that sharp ache.

That mixture of longing and guilt, breathlessness and shame that seemed fused to her bones.

And yet looking at him was a balm as much as it sometimes felt like a punishment—because she knew she didn't deserve this man. Even from her vantage point, she could *feel* that air of command and certainty he wore the way other men wore their shirts. She could see the way the others looked to him, leaped to do his bidding, and always seemed pleased to be near him.

She was familiar with those sentiments.

The whole world knew that Pau Calixto was a good man. He had made his straightforwardness and moral code central to his success. He had made it clear that there were no skeletons in his closet, nor ever would be.

This was why her father had worked so hard to rehabilitate her brother's image, thinking it would convince Pau that the Tavian family was not as reprehensible as most assumed thanks to Giaco's behavior. And Umberto's behavior, Leontina had thought—though had never dared say—because no one who'd met the man had anything nice to say about him unless they wanted something from him.

It was almost poetic that she was the one who had come along and put Pau's moral goodness to the test, she thought. Maybe the snide papers had been right all along when they'd talked about the Tavian family's deep rot within—they'd just got the wrong sibling.

Then again, she hadn't spent that night in the castle alone.

Maybe Pau was as human as everyone else. Maybe *she* was his weakness.

Leontina couldn't help but like that notion, tangled

though it was with her enduring guilt over making all of this happen in the first place.

She blew out a breath and turned away from the window, wrapping herself in the dress he'd taken such pleasure in unraveling from her body last night. It was a wrap dress, it accentuated every curve on her body, and Pau had been deeply—ravenously—appreciative. His appreciation had begun during the intimate dinner they'd shared and had moved quickly here, to his bed.

Where they had stayed awake far later than they should have.

Yet she couldn't regret it.

She thought that perhaps she ought to talk to him about different sorts of practical things. Like, given the fact they slept together every night, actually moving herself into his bedroom instead of trekking back and forth from the opposite end of the sprawling old house.

But she could admit to herself, as she took the long walk back to her wing of the house, that she wasn't comfortable doing that. It wasn't going to happen. How could she install herself in the man's bedroom—and no matter that he'd married her—when she knew that no matter what, she was essentially here under false pretenses?

Pau persisted in believing he had seduced an innocent. And yes, she'd been a virgin. But that didn't mean that there had been any seducing. Not on his part.

To think I have turned an innocent into such a wanton, he had whispered into the heat of her skin one night as she sat astride him, taking him in deep and rocking herself toward that wildfire bliss that was becoming something of an addiction. *Who could have believed it of a girl who used to pride herself on disappearing in crowded rooms?*

It was a theme he returned to again and again, now that he'd surrendered to the passion between them. Now that he'd decided that their nights—all of their nights—were to be spent together.

Now that he'd made it clear that the fire between them had been no fluke at her brother's wedding.

Look at you burn, he had growled on another night. *It's like you were made for me, Leontina. What would have become of all this heat if I had not led you so far astray?*

Some nights she almost convinced herself that he was taunting her, poking at her, possibly even *trying* to get a reaction, almost as if he knew the truth—

But she dismissed that. Every morning she woke up, feeling deliciously burned through all over and desperate for more, and she told herself that was only her guilty conscience talking. Because if he knew, she wouldn't have to confess. If he knew and was still happy to lose himself in this fire together, then maybe it was all right—

And Leontina knew full well that it was not.

She merely wished it was.

As she walked through the monastery, she murmured reassuring words to the baby with every step, because that part, at least, was real. And maybe once the baby was born, she would worry less about how she'd come to be here in the first place. Because surely all that would matter then was the child.

Leontina was sure of it.

She was thinking of that a few days later when Pau

drove her down into Tarragona again, this time to pay a visit to a doctor he knew who was an OB-GYN in the city and who he'd called to give Leontina a full examination.

A doctor who he apparently knew well, she discovered.

"Assumpció could have gone anywhere," Pau told her as he drove. "She studied at some of the finest institutions in the world. But, like me, she was born in this region and was determined to return here, to get back to it. To put her talents to use here, where they will matter more because she was made here."

"She sounds like quite the paragon," Leontina said, and only realized once the words were out that she sounded…perhaps a bit sharper than planned.

Pau's dark eyes gleamed as he cast a look at her, then returned his attention to the road.

"Perhaps I have not yet mentioned the most salient point about Assumpció," he said. "She is not only one of my oldest friends. She is also my cousin." And she could hear the *excessive* mildness in his voice as he continued. "In case there were any misunderstandings on that score."

Leontina felt…embarrassed, maybe. Her cheeks were hot and there was a dark, throbbing sort of thread of emotion curling tight inside her—but she couldn't identify it.

Or she didn't want to, more like.

"I don't know what you mean," she managed to say.

"Of course you don't," Pau replied, but she was sure that she could hear the very faintest hint of laughter in that tone of his.

Somehow, that made it worth it. It made that darkness in her settle.

And then, of course, Assumpció was a delight. She was irreverent with Pau, warm and direct with Leontina, and when it was time for the ultrasound, she made it all seem easy and natural and even comfortable.

Lying on that table, her feet in stirrups, Leontina thought that really, this was the point where she ought to have been embarrassed. There could not be anything more inelegant than lying like this while a stranger bustled around and everyone pretended that Leontina's most private parts were not on display.

But somehow, that wasn't how it felt at all.

And as she lay there, she felt a strange sensation inside her. Like a wriggling—and then, in the very same moment she asked herself what it was, she knew the answer.

Without thinking, she reached out and grabbed Pau's hand, then pressed it to her belly with its little bump.

"The baby is kicking," she told him excitedly. "Can you feel it?"

She glanced up to find him looking startled, his dark eyes blazing gold. The baby kicked again then, even harder, and both of them seemed to break into the same smile at once.

And for all the wildly hot nights they'd shared, all the positions they'd tried, and the ecstasy they'd eked out of each other's bodies, Leontina couldn't help thinking that this was a far greater intimacy than any of them. It was a different, simpler joy.

It was theirs in a way that felt deeply rooted in both

of them, and she could feel it in the warmth of his palm against her belly.

"Do you want to know the baby's sex?" Assumpció asked quietly, somehow not breaking into the moment, but deepening it.

Leontina couldn't tear her gaze away from Pau's. She could see his answer there. Slowly, she nodded, too.

"Yes," Pau said quietly. "We would."

"It is my pleasure and privilege to tell you that you will be having a little boy," Assumpció told them. "A perfect little boy, by all current measurements. As happy and healthy as anyone could wish." She looked at Leontina then. "You are doing beautifully."

Then the doctor excused herself from the room. It took Leontina long moments to slowly realize that she was lying there in nothing but a hospital gown, with Pau's hand a blaze of heat, a sweet and heavy weight on her belly.

And it never would have occurred to her that a clinical moment like this could be so many other things as well. That so many emotions could be involved. That the air itself could feel *layered* with things too dangerous to speak out loud.

There was the heat of his hand and the way her body responded to that, and to him, and that physical connection of theirs that only seemed to deepen—and even more so today. It was like the heat wound its way into her and made her glow.

There was that look in his eyes, somehow tender and arresting at once.

And she could not stop thinking how magical and bizarre it was that a night that had seemed so decadent, so vulnerable, so *wicked*, could lead to something as pure as the baby she carried and the shivery, delicious complication of this moment they shared together.

They had enjoyed each other so thoroughly that they had left marks on each other's skin, but they'd also made a whole *life*.

That made something in her crack wide open.

"Pau," she said, her voice little more than a whisper, "I have to tell you—"

"I will wait outside while you dress," he told her, quietly.

And Leontina lay there, awash in something like misery—but sharper—once he left.

Maybe this was the price she had to pay, as simple as that. Maybe she was just going to have to live with this. It was a sort of tax she would have to pay again and again in moments like this, because of *how* she'd done this. Because of what she'd done and how she'd let it carry on this long.

She told herself that there was no such thing as perfect happiness, and she was a fool to imagine that if she only came clean, she and Pau could achieve it.

And maybe it was nothing more than selfishness in the first place that made her want to tell him the truth. Because what could he do about it anyway? Nothing could change what had happened.

The only thing that could change was that he might make her feel better about it, somehow, and Leontina knew she had to let that go. Because it was also possible that her confession could make things worse, and that wasn't fair to the baby.

She was going to have to find a way to come to terms

with the fact that she'd done what she'd done for the right reasons, no matter if anyone else thought she was right to do it. And if she had any emotional reaction to that, well, that was something she would have to forge through on her own.

It wasn't that she was unused to figuring things out for herself. It was that these last weeks with Pau had made her realize how much better everything was when she was not left entirely to her own devices.

When she wasn't alone.

Going back to the way things had been before...hurt.

"Just focus on the baby," she told herself beneath her breath as she tidied herself up, used the bathroom, and pulled her clothes back on. "On our son."

And it was like those were magic words. Her son. *Their* son.

A little boy who she could already, suddenly, envision as if he was standing there before her. Perhaps he would have the same dark green eyes she and her brother did, maybe even ringed with gold like his father's. He was certain to have dark hair, and she wondered if he'd be born with that look of a stamped old coin, like all the generations of Calixtos who'd come before him, as if their history was so intense it showed on their cheeks.

She wondered if she'd see herself in him. Or perhaps she'd see her mother—like the beautiful ghost she sometimes seemed to glimpse out of the corner of her eye when she turned away from a mirror.

A little boy, she thought, letting the joy of that wash through her as she walked out of the exam room. She smiled when she saw Dr. Assumpció in the outer office.

"Pau has gone on ahead," the other woman told her. "I believe he's pulling the car around. But I have to tell you, this is like a miracle."

Leontina laughed. "I assure you it is not. We got pregnant in the very unmiraculous, usual way."

Though it had felt a bit like a miracle to her, if she was honest. It still did. Every time.

Assumpció laughed, too. "I don't mean that. Believe me, I know where babies come from. I mean Pau. I've never seen him like this."

There was, of course, nothing on earth Leontina wanted to hear more than stories about how Pau was besotted with her and a changed man in every regard, but she really didn't think that was the case.

Still, she couldn't help but smile and lean a little closer. "Like what?" she asked. "Married, you mean?"

"That part, sure," Assumpció said, laughter in her gaze. "And his choice of bride is fascinating, of course. I knew that he was friends with your brother at university, but we all thought that he cut Giaco off years ago because of his…" She clearly recalled who she was speaking to and abruptly cut herself off. "They are very different people, is what I mean to say."

"Indeed they are," Leontina agreed.

Pau's cousin looked faintly flustered, now. "I seem to be stumbling left and right, and I already have a foot in my mouth. Possibly both feet." She inclined her head. "All I want to say is that the only thing I've ever known Pau to be intense about, and intently focused on, is the vineyard. When we were kids, I always thought he would have burned every vine to the ground if he could, but everything changed after my uncle died.

Pau became obsessed with the company. To a concerning degree. I'm both surprised and delighted that he's broadened his scope. That's all I meant."

"That is how I received it," Leontina assured her. "Why do you think he changed so dramatically?"

Maybe it was a foolish question to ask his cousin. Or too intimate when she'd only just met the woman. But Assumpció nodded as if it was a reasonable follow-up.

"My mother and I have always believed that it is the only way he can feel close to Bernat now," she said quietly. "By loving what his father loved, perhaps?" The other woman smiled. "But you know him far better, I think. You would be better equipped to know the truth of this."

Leontina's mind was spinning as she left the office and made her way out the old, cobbled street, where Pau stood beside the gleaming SUV he'd driven here.

Because she wasn't sure that she did know Pau better than his cousin. And she thought that she should. More than that, she wanted—desperately—to know him inside and out, the way she knew his body now.

It felt like a kind of madness to want someone this much.

She felt the moment his gaze landed on her, and all that dark focus of his centered on her alone, as if they were entirely isolated on this Spanish street when she knew they were not. Just like the first time, just like every time, it was like being struck by lightning. Leontina smiled, and as she did, had the overwhelming sense that everything was changed now. That she was walking out of that office a different woman from the one who'd walked in.

When the baby moved inside her, she understood.

Up until this moment, she'd been pregnant. It had been something that was happening to her, though she spoke to the baby and sang it songs—but most of her thoughts about the future were loose. Vague. She'd been a pregnant woman carrying a child who was still mostly abstract.

Today she'd become a mother. Just as Pau had become a father. They had become the parents of the little boy they would meet in just under half a year from now.

It was all a good deal more real than it had seemed this morning. Their son had taken shape, and in so doing, changed the shape of everything around him.

No wonder this all felt sacred.

No wonder this need to *know* the man she shared her body and her child with felt so desperate.

Pau did not speak. Leontina could feel all that electricity simmering in him and crackling in her, too, as he opened the passenger door for her. Then he took her hand as he helped her inside, though she didn't require assistance. She thought she might have refused it on any other day.

But today was special.

And it was like the world stopped for a moment. She felt as if they froze in place. He could have held her hand for an hour, a day, a lifetime. When, realistically, it couldn't have been more than a few scant seconds.

He pulled away and closed the door, and for a moment she sat alone in the warm interior of the car with everything inside her a jumble of sensation, emotion, and something far more dangerous, like hope.

It stuck with her even though he barely spoke a word on the drive back to the vineyard.

That night, he sent word that he would not meet her for dinner in another new dining room, as was their usual custom.

Leontina took a tray in her rooms and felt rather more philosophical about it than she might have on another night. She understood. Everything now was shaped like a small baby boy they had yet to meet. To her it was so simple. Almost funny.

They'd had so much sex and yet it was a few quiet moments marinating in the realization that they were having a son together that had knocked everything sideways.

She supposed it made sense that he needed a moment to calibrate.

Maybe she should be grateful, she thought. Maybe this was nothing more than an excellent opportunity for her to catch up on her sleep.

She crawled into bed early and dreamed of him, and then, later, woke up when she felt the mattress bend beneath the weight of another body.

"Pau," she murmured sleepily. "What are you—"

"You're giving me a child," he said fiercely. "My true legacy, Leontina."

And the way he kissed her then set her soul on fire.

The way he touched her took her outside herself entirely.

He was slow, unhurried. He took his time, pulling off the nightclothes she wore and murmuring his appreciation at the roundness of her breasts, the swell of her belly. And as he settled between her legs, holding them open with his wide shoulders, the sound he made was one of simple, stark male approval.

And then he set his mouth to the core of her and licked her straight off the precipice, sending her streaking out into the night like a comet.

One orgasm wasn't enough. She cried out, and shook all around him, and he simply began again. And then again, adding his fingers, turning his head to press kisses to her shaking thighs—and the odd nip that seemed to keep her trembling right there on the edge.

She was both outside herself and never more firmly in her own body when he shifted again. He rolled so he could strip off the lounging trousers he wore, then came back over her to pull her legs up high and set them upon his shoulders so he could slide in deep.

His cock seemed bigger than before, or maybe she was simply over-sensitized tonight, because with one stroke she was nearly there. Another, and she was flying

Pau only laughed, settled in, and kept going.

And the whole of the world narrowed down to the pace he set. The way his strong hands wrapped around her legs to keep her in place as he plunged deep inside her, sending her spinning out with no focus at all but the fire in his dark gaze.

Like they were one. Like there was nothing between them, nor ever could be, but this connection. This heat. This wildfire that had been theirs from the very start.

It was the opposite of loneliness. It was an intense searching, a communion, a new wholeness.

When she broke again, she screamed.

Pau heard her and it seemed to inflame him, because his thrusts became less measured, less sure. He pulled her legs apart and came down between them, holding himself up on his elbows so that he was not crushing her belly.

It was so deep, so perfect, so *good* that she felt herself shoot back up to that precipice. And when he released himself deep inside her with a roar, she felt the scalding heat of it, and joined him.

Leontina woke again in the gloom of the predawn. For a moment, she didn't know what woke her. She felt disoriented until she saw Pau sitting at the end of the bed, his head bent down.

She felt scraped hollow then, as she watched him. And she didn't know why she didn't reach out. Why she didn't tell him she was awake.

He looked so lonely. He looked the way she sometimes felt, and the way she so deeply had not felt yesterday that it actually hurt her to think it was possible that he could feel that way right now.

Maybe she was frozen into staying still.

Whatever it was, Leontina didn't move until he got up—eventually—and padded silently out of her room. She didn't move until she heard his footsteps fade away, down the hallway, headed back across the old house again.

And then she *couldn't* move, because she felt swamped with self-recrimination. Because she couldn't help but think they ought to have been falling in love. That they might have been.

But the fact remained that she was a liar on a fundamental level.

And clearly Pau knew that—whether consciously

or unconsciously—because that had not been the demeanor of a happy, expectant father.

Leontina hated herself, and that was no new feeling.

Her father had made it clear that she was to blame for her mother's death, and maybe this was why. Maybe Umberto had been uniquely positioned to see exactly what sort of terrible person his daughter was, because he'd watched what she'd done to her own mother.

She felt the tears come and she wiped them away furiously, because she didn't deserve them. How could she live with herself now, knowing that this, too, was her fault? How could she live with herself knowing—even worse—that because of her manipulations, she was really no better than her father after all?

When she'd been so *certain* that she was better?

This had all seemed like a reasonable game to play, once upon a time. She'd wanted an escape plan. Pau had been an excellent candidate. It had helped that she'd felt an instant attraction to him when she'd seen him.

Now he was not only her husband, and her lover, but the father of their son.

None of it seemed *reasonable* anymore.

She tried to go back to sleep, resolved that she would go ahead and tell him the truth, because it had to be better for it all to be out in the open. Even if he hated her for a time, she thought he might come around eventually, and at least that way they would be built on something real. Not these lies.

Surely it would be worth blowing everything up if it meant they could start fresh and become *real*.

But in the days that followed, there never seemed to be a good time to tell him. The harvest took all of his attention during the day and when he came to her it was in the dark, late at night, and the wild passion between them seemed at a fever point.

She thought maybe she was at her fever point too, or maybe she was simply a coward, because she couldn't seem to bring herself to throw a bomb into the middle of things as they were.

Leontina told herself that the slower seasons would come soon enough, and she would find the right moment there. In the quiet. In the cold before their child was born.

Maybe then it would be the sort of bomb they'd survive.

It was the beginning of her second month in Spain, halfway through October, when a different bomb altogether strolled into the old monastery, charmed his way past the staff who should have been better prepared to hold off intruders—even the sparkling kind—and walked in on Leontina and Pau as they shared one of their dinners. This night they were clustered close together on a small balcony, festooned everywhere with lantern light, in defiance of the chill in the air.

"How cozy," said Giaco, lounging bonelessly in the entryway, his eyes that were so like Leontina's taking in the scene. Leontina herself was frozen solid.

She thought it was something like panic.

"I've heard the most extraordinary rumor," her brother continued when neither one of them managed to offer a greeting. "I usually ignore anything that comes out of our father's appalling mouth. But he did insist that in defiance of all logic, my biddable, obedient sister had finally run away from his tender ministrations and paternal devotion. This seemed unlikely enough. Imagine my surprise, when I convinced Umberto's security detail to tell me what they'd found when they investigated it, that all signs seemed to indicate that my baby sister was shacked up with my best friend in what I can only imagine—for my sanity and your continued ability to draw breath, Pau—is a deeply platonic relationship. They have, naturally, decided to delay telling my father this until someone could come in person and lo, I nominated myself to be that person."

His gaze dropped, almost lazily, to where Pau had taken Leontina's hand over the table some while ago to fiddle with the wedding rings he'd put there, as had become his habit.

Leontina couldn't breathe. Pau seemed to have gone to stone.

But her brother, as always, was not similarly encumbered.

"Tell me," Giaco said, with a smile that went nowhere near his eyes, too intensely focused were they on his best friend in all the world, "why I shouldn't I kill you here and now? *Brother?*"

CHAPTER SIX

Pᴀᴜ ꜱᴛᴏᴏᴅ ɪᴍᴍᴇᴅɪᴀᴛᴇʟʏ. It felt as if he'd been beset by some terrible, sudden onset arthritis like the kind that had plagued his grandmother in the end. It made the whole of his body ache. It made him wonder for a moment if his legs would hold beneath him and keep him upright.

Maybe there was a part of him that wished he truly would collapse—and the cowardice in that notion almost knocked him sideways all on its own.

Because the truth was, he had always known this moment would come. He had simply wished there would be more time before it arrived. He'd wanted the child to be here in the world with them, the better to take his little family before her father to show him how fully and completely the old man had lost his grip.

How useless his little plots were.

How pointless he was, in the end—the way that he'd made Bernat feel.

Pau supposed that somewhere on the other side of all that, he'd imagined that he and Giaco would meet and discuss what had happened. The new future that Pau had created thanks to Leontina. The final nail in

Umberto's living coffin. Complete with a new addition to Giaco's family—sugar to sweeten a bitter pill.

He had certainly not expected that this would all happen *tonight*.

His entire body *hurt*, yet he knew perfectly well it was not arthritis. He had a good idea what else it could be, and all of it earned. Shame. Guilt. Regret.

The consequences of his actions in the decidedly human form of his best friend, who was currently looking at him as if he'd like to kill him. With his bare hands.

The way Pau had known all along he would, one day.

Pau was tempted to let him.

Maybe if Giaco took a few swings at him, it would ease the tension enough that the two of them could have a conversation. It wasn't as if Giaco was a stranger to using relationships to further his own ends. The last ten years or so of his own life told that story eloquently enough, as did his very tactical and strategic marriage—the one he'd let his father believe he was forcing Giaco into.

No one had expected that Giaco and his forced bride, who also happened to be his former stepsister, Ivy, would fall in love.

Yet, somehow, Pau knew better than to bring that up. Just as—*somehow*—he understood that Giaco would not view his sister as fair game in the kind of sport they'd both indulged in all these years. Not that Giaco had ever declared Leontina off-limits, but then, he would have assumed that was unnecessary.

"Giaco," he said warmly, in greeting, as he always did. "Brother." He did not say that last part ironically, and he watched his friend's brow rise. Perhaps it shouldn't have been shocking how much that felt like a strike straight into his solar plexus. "Perhaps you and I should step inside for a small moment."

"There's nothing you can't say in front of me," Leontina argued, scowling at her brother. She looked as displeased to see him as Giaco was with Pau.

"I was friends with your brother first," Pau told her, as evenly as possible. And he did not take his eyes off Giaco. He wasn't that foolish. "I owe him this much."

"I would say you owe me this *at the very least*," Giaco interjected, sounding almost merry—though his dark green eyes were still dark. "If I start to make a list of the things I think you owe me in this moment, my dear friend, we will become voluminous within seconds."

But he didn't make any move to lunge at Pau's throat, so that was something.

Pau inclined his head. He looked at Leontina, who gazed back at him with mutiny in her gaze. Her chin rose up, belligerently, but as he gazed at her, she lowered it again. Eventually she blew out a breath, and nodded.

He felt a rush of another one of these dark, overwhelming emotions that swamped him every time he looked at her. He did not pretend to know what they were.

But it took greater effort than perhaps it should have to tear his gaze away from her, and follow her brother back into the monastery.

Giaco roamed bonelessly into the room, as was his custom, somehow eating it up with a glance. Pau closed the door to the balcony behind him, made sure it was shut tight so Leontina need not hear any of what was about to come, and waited.

He watched his always larger-than-life friend as Giaco put on a small performance of casually wandering about the room, taking in the stylized details and modern flourishes as if he had wandered into a museum somewhere, before he looked back at Pau.

"Who knew there was such a thing as Catholic chic?" he asked with a mildness that Pau did not believe at all.

"I forget you've never been here before." Pau chose to ignore the undercurrents entirely. "Having heard so much about this place over the years, I trust you have found it exactly as described."

"Save for the serpent nestled within," Giaco replied, as swiftly as a knife strike deep into Pau's gut. His dark eyes blazed. "What the fuck, Pau?"

Pau had known this man for nearly half his life. They had met and bonded as teenagers let loose in the august university where Pau had been expected to excel, and Giaco had intended to—and succeeded in—living down the lowest expectations of anyone who encountered him, particularly if they knew his father.

Theirs had always been the sort of friendship that defied explanation. Pau had considered it often in the intervening years. There was something about the people a person met the first time they were on their own. The first time they were out in the world, playing at adulthood on their own. There was something about those bonds.

Or there was something about this one. Because even after Giaco was summarily sent down from university in the middle of their first year, they had stayed in touch. Even when Pau had started his life of respectability and duty while Giaco chased starlets through glittering parties all over the globe, they had remained close.

And after his father died, when Pau had discovered who had engineered that death, Giaco had been his first call.

You know I've always hated that miserable excuse for a man, Giaco had said with a quiet ferocity after Pau had laid out all the facts he'd uncovered, yet could not prove in any sort of way that would hurt Umberto. *Now I detest him even more.*

Pau had not known until that moment how deeply he had needed his friend to believe him. Or how certain he had been that in the moment of truth, Giaco would close down and protect his family rather than his friend. But he hadn't.

Nor did he ever.

Instead, the two of them had crafted a long-term plan to destroy Umberto from within. They would each lean into their strengths. Giaco, already a prolific despoiler of women, had catapulted himself into internationally renowned infamy. Pau, who rarely attracted any notice, had certainly gained some in the wake of his father's death—and he'd leaned into that. Because it was up to him to rebuild Calixto Estates for the sake of his father's honor and also to use it to lure Umberto back in.

Because if Umberto had wanted Calixto once, they were certain that he would want it again when it was worth even more.

They'd been right about that.

It had taken over a decade, but they had finally taken

the old man out at the knees in a boardroom in Madrid, where Umberto had believed that he and the supposedly ultra-virtuous Pau were signing a deal that would deeply enrich Umberto's coffers. The old man had expected the deal to keep him sitting pretty into his dotage.

Instead, Giaco had stepped in, revealing himself as a secret partner in the business all along, and cutting Umberto out in a way that would not render the man destitute—that was simply a pipe dream, given his wealth—but had humbled him. Embarrassed him. And had significantly decreased his net worth.

The good news was, they did not have to bankrupt Umberto to hurt him. He was too used to his billions. Having only *millions* made him desperate.

It would be pathetic if it wasn't so well-deserved.

And all of that, Pau understood as he looked at his best friend's face, was nothing to Giaco in this moment. Because on the other side of the plated glass doors sat Giaco's sister. Who should never have become involved in any of this. Who was in no way Giaco's detested father.

Who Pau should certainly never, ever have touched. Much less with the express intention of using her as a weapon in this long war of theirs.

He'd known this all along. He'd also known that this reckoning could not be avoided. Not forever.

"I cannot defend myself," Pau told his friend as evenly as he could. "But I will explain."

"I do not need your explanations," Giaco threw back at him. "It's obvious to me what you're doing at a glance. We've lived on revenge for more than ten years,

Pau. I recognize it when I see it. What I cannot understand is why you did it behind my back."

"Because I knew that you would not permit it to happen if I told you that I was doing it," Pau retorted. Starkly. "And yet it is something that needed to happen, I am afraid."

"It *needed to happen*?" Giaco echoed him, then shook his head. "You needed to lure my sister from the only home she has ever known, transport her across borders, and install her in your creepy little convent—"

"The house was, in fact, a monastery."

Giaco shook his head, though his dark gaze remained hard. "My sister is truly the only innocent I believe I have ever met," he bit out. "Certainly the only one in the Tavian family. And you know that very well, old friend. You know it as well as I do. One can only assume that this was the point."

"Your father did not simply destroy my family business," Pau threw back at his friend, his voice something less than even as it shook with the force of that dark and vicious emotion he held for the man he had long considered his enemy. His nemesis. "That was bad enough. The legacy of my family was *this close* to being wiped from the earth, and for what? One old, rich, morally destitute man's ego?"

"So you chose to morally bankrupt yourself in response, and at my sister's expense?" Giaco looked at him with an astonishment that Pau did not think was remotely feigned. "This from a man *heralded* across Europe for his virtuous center that defines every choice he makes?"

"I am as much a saint as you are a devil," Pau

growled. "We have both used these reputations to our advantage, have we not?"

"I don't recall prancing into your family in all my state and systematically dismantling your siblings, and not only because you don't have any." Giaco's mouth thinned. "You, on the other hand, did that and more. A wolf in the manger, when the manger was already heaving with wolves aplenty. Quite an accomplishment, Pau, to out-wolf the kind of people who were at my wedding, where I assume you met her. A thieves' gallery of the world's worst, and yet you've given them all a run for their money."

That was a blow, and Pau didn't pretend it didn't land. But he pushed on anyway.

"I will tell you this," he managed to say with some remnant of his usual equanimity. "I would lose every single vine that was planted by the hard labor of my ancestors if it meant my father was still here. He's not like your father, Giaco. Or like me. He truly was a good man. An honorable man. He lived by his own moral code and held himself to high standards expected from everyone around him, including me." He forced himself to breathe, and not to look away, because he felt perilously close to the emotions he had been trained out of expressing as a child, and he could not see how they would help here. "And your father deliberately and systematically stripped him of everything that was meaningful to him. His legacy. His honor. And yes, eventually, his life."

Not to mention any chance Pau might have had to understand his father better. Or get to know him when he was older and, perhaps, a bit softer.

He tried to shove such unruly notions aside.

"I know all this," Giaco threw back at him. "What I don't know is how you decided that you should make *my sister* pay for my father's sins. I thought that you and I had taken on that challenge. What did Leontina ever do to you?"

That, it turned out, was a far more loaded question than it should have been. But this was not the time or place to discuss the great many things Leontina had done to him, and all of them incapacitating in ways that Pau was not at all certain he was likely to recover from.

"She is my wife," he said quietly. Intently. "And come the winter, she will be the mother of my son. These are the only facts that matter."

Pau watched that go through Giaco like an electric current, confirming to him that Giaco did not know about the pregnancy. That he was here because he knew his sister had come here. This meant that he might not know that they were married, either.

He watched his friend go incandescent, and he could feel the violence of it, though Giaco did not in fact lunge across the room the way Pau half thought—and half hoped, perhaps—he would. Pau thought he could see the exact moment that Giaco counted the correct number of months, and came to the inevitable conclusion.

He'd already understood that Leontina and Pau had *met* at his wedding. Now he knew what else had gone on.

Giaco looked murderous.

"I'm not one to descend into violence," his friend said in a low, furious voice, "no matter how much I'd like to indulge the urge to punch you in the face."

Pau thought better of commenting on that. This was not the Giaco he'd known for years. This was not his friend—always more intense than the world believed but fundamentally good. This was a man who would have no compunction defending his sister, and Pau could not help but love him for that. Because surely, someone should have defended Leontina all along.

It was not lost on him that her life had been no easier than his. He had thought so even before she'd pointed out how little choice he'd had along the way.

Giaco was still speaking. "I'm also entirely too familiar with the impossibility of denying both passion and emotion," he said, making Pau think about Giaco's own marriage. About the farce it had been at first, or had been supposed to be. And what it was now—the true love match between Giaco and a woman who was referred to as *Saint Ivy* in the press, and was highly celebrated for seemingly taming the wildest of beastly men in Giaco.

Pau knew that truly, she had.

And he wanted to argue with Giaco about the words he'd chosen. *Passion. Emotion.* But somehow, he couldn't bring himself to do it.

Maybe because they'd been speaking of his father, who had never told a lie. And therefore Pau could not bring himself to tell one now. Not to the only real, true friend he'd ever had.

"I truly want to understand," Giaco was saying. "And while I have been called many things and know myself to be far more and much worse, I hope I'm not a hypocrite. I cannot possibly blame you for actions I'm quite certain I would have taken myself." His dark jade eyes, so much like his sister's, bored into Pau. "I must also tell you that if she sheds so much as a single tear in my presence tonight, there will be a reckoning."

It was quiet between them, then. The quiet seemed to stretch out, encompassing too many years, too many plans, the great revenge scheme they had already pulled off. And perhaps even those early days, when they'd been lanky, unformed teenagers sharing a stair at Cambridge and had started some stilted conversation lost in time one night. Then had taken to sloping about ancient courtyards, feeling invincible and overwhelmed at once.

He looked past Giaco to where Leontina had moved and was standing, looking out into the dark. He both knew her better now and yet felt at times that he knew her not at all. She stood with her spine straight. And he could tell that she was fighting her emotions even from the back. He knew every noise she made, every whisper, every sigh. He knew a hundred different ways she said his name. Sobbed it. Shouted. Cried it out.

And he also knew what Giaco clearly did not, which was that innocent though she may have been, his sister was no sheltered little nun. She'd had every intention of falling pregnant by his hands—or by his cock, to be more precise—and had made sure that it happened.

Then had come here, likely as certain as anyone could be that the wildly virtuous Pau Calixto would, of course, do the honorable thing.

It was lowering to think that even if Pau hadn't intended to seduce her himself, he very likely would have fallen captive to her that night all the same.

He could not tell this to his friend. He could not explain what had happened to him when Leontina Tavian had looked at him with a boldness he'd never seen on her face before, walked over to him in that stunning dress she'd worn on Giaco's wedding day, and had smiled directly at him. When she'd moved closer and asked him if he was having fun.

Then put her hand on his arm and set him on fire.

He doubted his friend would believe him.

"I don't mean to be provocative," he said, carefully. But with perfect honesty. "But Giaco, I do not think you know your sister at all."

He expected that to enrage his friend. But Giaco surprised him, lifting only a shoulder though his eyes remained hard on Pau.

"That is highly possible," he agreed. "I don't pretend to be someone other than who I am. Nor the older brother she deserved. But that does not make me any more kindly disposed to you and your secretive campaign to know her biblically, either."

Pau understood. "Then you must speak to her and satisfy yourself," he said.

Giaco nodded. He moved toward Pau, and perhaps neither one of them knew if he would take a swing or not—but he didn't.

Instead, Giaco kept going and opened up the doors to the balcony again.

"Leontina," Giaco called to his sister. "Come inside."

Leontina turned and walked toward them, a wary sort of look on her face.

"Let me guess," she said. "This is yet another example of men getting together and deciding my life and future without any input from me. Do either one of you have any idea what it is like to be—"

But when she reached the door, still speaking, Giaco pulled her close and hugged her, hard.

Pau was standing behind them, so he saw as Leontina first stiffened, looking shocked. How her mouth shut with a snap, then fell open again.

And then, as Giaco continued to hug her, how she shook. Until her whole face crumpled, punching a hole straight through Pau's chest.

It was no surprise to him when she began to sob.

Giaco held her, murmuring things in Italian. He turned, very slowly, to send a cold, hard look Pau's way. When Leontina pulled away, Giaco shook his head.

"I told you," he said. "I warned you, did I not? *Brother*."

And then he wound up, swung, and laid Pau out on his own floor.

CHAPTER SEVEN

In the pantheon of things that Leontina had imagined might happen that day, Giaco appearing at all—much less to give her a *hug* and then follow that up by getting into an actual fistfight with Pau—would not even have made the top hundred possibilities she might have come up with.

At first, it was as if she couldn't comprehend what she was seeing.

Because it didn't make sense. Her brother was the life of every party. A bright sort of beaming creature whose primary weapons were his words and his insinuations—not his fists. She would have said he didn't have it in him to throw a punch at anyone.

Yet here they were.

Leontina stood, frozen into place, as the two men engaged in a fistfight on the floor.

Though she retracted that word as soon as she thought it. It wasn't a *fight*. Pau was letting Giaco hit him. He wasn't doing anything to fight back, and was only barely defending himself. It seemed her brother lost his taste for waling on a man who threw no punches himself, and fast.

"Asshole," Giaco muttered, rolling off his best friend and then slumping there on the floor beside him.

The two of them lay there a while, breathing more heavily than usual.

By contrast, Leontina could hardly breathe at all. In fact, she didn't think her nose was working the way it should have be—

She realized belatedly that she was sobbing.

But not because she was sad or upset. She was sobbing because she was *furious*.

She was outraged that they were fighting for her honor without even discussing it with her. She was furious that they had *moved into another room* to discuss *their feelings* about the decisions she'd made about *her life*.

And the fact that her older brother had finally shown that he cared didn't make it any better. Not now.

None of these competing furies diminished any as Pau rolled gracefully to his feet, then brushed himself off without seeming to be the slightest bit interested in the fact that he had a bloodied lip. To say nothing of what looked like the beginnings of a black eye.

And more intense emotion on his face than Leontina had ever seen there. Nothing cold. Nothing measured. Under different circumstances, she might have stopped and stared.

But this was not the moment for that sort of thing. Not with her brother here, messing with the delicate balance that she and Pau had managed to keep in place since she'd come to Calixto Estates to inform him about his paternity.

This was not the moment to ask her husband what

could put that look on his face. What could make him *simmer* and *shine* with things she didn't know how to name—

Or why, when his gaze met hers, he swallowed hard. Then let all that intensity fade away.

A lot like he locked it up somewhere inside him, but she couldn't follow that line of thought, either.

Not right now.

"Are you satisfied?" Pau demanded of Giaco, turning his dark gaze on her brother and letting it stay there. "Because I don't intend to do this again. So if you are not, this is your moment. This is your *only* moment."

Giaco only sighed, and muttered a quiet *yes* with a few choice insults appended to the end. In three separate languages, for effect.

"I cannot argue with you on your character assessments," Pau said darkly. "My brother."

And then, without so much as a glance in Leontina's direction, he stalked off, out of the room.

Leontina could not stop crying. *Snuffling* and crying, and it only made her angrier.

"Leontina," Giaco began, though he did not bother to rise from the ground.

"You've never hugged me in your entire life!" Leontina threw at him, letting her voice do what it would. Which in this case was to threaten the chandelier above them. "Why would you do it now?"

For the first time in as long as she'd known him, which was her whole entire life since the day she was born, her older brother looked…nonplussed. Uncertain.

If she'd been less furious, it might have concerned her.

Then she thought of Pau's perfect face, marred by

Giaco's hands that no one had asked him to throw. And she found she was not terribly concerned at all.

"You looked like you needed it," her brother said. In a quiet sort of voice that was nothing like his usual performative *theatrics* at all.

"Really, Giaco?" She still couldn't stop crying. And while she thought it was probably the pregnancy hormones making things extra-chaotic, as far as she could tell they only amplified her existing emotions, so there was that. She angrily wiped at her eyes. "Don't you think I might have *needed it* before? Don't you think a hug might have helped me while I was a motherless girl navigating Umberto's bullshit all by myself? Or were you too busy making yourself even more famous than you already were to worry overmuch about what was happening back at the castle you got away from as fast as you possibly could?"

Giaco's mouth actually dropped open.

But Leontina wasn't done. "I know she died because of me," she said, throwing out that ugly little truth about their lost mother that she'd been carrying her whole life. "But you have to know it wasn't really my fault. You didn't have to hate me too, just because he does."

Giaco looked as if she'd struck him, maybe taken one of the ornamental swords off the wall and used it to stab him straight through the heart.

"I *protected* you!" he belted out, sounding slightly outraged. "Umberto loves nothing more than to destroy anything and everything that strays across his path, or have you forgotten that? Do you really think you'd have survived and *thrived* enough to enact your escape if I hadn't created an enduring distraction? You do me a disservice."

Leontina shook her head. "All I remember is that you *actually* disappeared while I had to learn how to *seem* to disappear while remaining in the room. But that's what she did, too, isn't it? First one, then the other. Is that our real family legacy?"

But somehow, when she got to the end of that sentence, she was less furious than when she started. It was like it all…blew away like so much smoke, and all that was left were the thorny emotions beneath.

And that wasn't fury. That was the mess that fury hid.

Giaco slowly rolled himself up and off the floor, displaying the easy athleticism that had done its part in making him more sought after than many of the more typical artsy celebrities of his generation. He went and sat on the low sofa that was stuck against one wall, beneath a giant canvas depicting some or other religious scene involving what looked like a spot of decapitation, in lustrous oils.

Leontina supposed she ought to recognize the painting, but she didn't. She sat below it on the same sofa as her brother, gingerly. She found herself thinking that it felt right, somehow, that they should be speaking of these ugly, heavy things they never talked about, here beneath a grand painting filled with blood and gore. That tracked, somehow.

"I never wanted you to feel like that," he said after they'd both settled on the couch, and he'd taken a moment to explore the state of his knuckles, looking raw after his exertions. "I went out of my way to make sure that you didn't."

"You didn't," she assured him. They were both looking straight ahead at the wall of weaponry, which, again, seemed fitting. It all seemed strange and yet right. "Not really. That was what Father always told me. That perhaps if I had been less disappointing, she would not have chosen to take her life."

Giaco made a low noise that Leontina wasn't sure she could identify. "What a foul, vicious man," he muttered. "You were six years old, Leontina. What could you have done?"

What an odd thing it was, she thought, to have one of the central questions of her existence thrown out like that—like a rhetorical question too absurd to require that she answer it. The sweep of swords and other bladed things she was certain had names, though she didn't know them, provided a kind of chorus. They seemed to pointedly underscore everything Giaco was saying.

"The truth is that our mother refused to diminish," Giaco said, intently. "She felt the cost was too high for her to meet, and I believe that she assumed—rightly—" and he flashed a look at her direction, as if he was calling her to account "—that you would be the same as she was in many ways. Inextinguishable. Indomitable. And yet better prepared than she could be to meet these challenges."

"I don't think anyone would describe me that way," Leontina replied softly. "Though it's lovely to imagine."

"I think you're selling yourself short," Giaco retorted. "You've lived with our father for more years than I ever did and have managed to avoid him for most of that time. Unless there are stories you've never told me about his coming after you over these past few years?" When Leontina shook her head, he nodded. She'd confirmed what he already thought. "I don't think that would be possible without the strongest spine and a will to match it. All that plus the sort of humility that allows you to go unseen in the first place. That's not me, certainly. And we both know that none of that comes from him."

She felt tears in her eyes again and she looked down at her hands, because, truly, she couldn't think of a greater gift he could have given her than to suggest that she was anything like their fierce, intimidating mother, who Umberto's acolytes still murmured about in hushed tones as if they expected her to rise from beyond and flay them into pieces as she'd apparently done nightly while she was here. Not one to suffer fools, even if it would have made her life easier—that was their mother.

But then, Giaco hadn't merely said that she was like their mother. He'd suggested that in some way, she was *better equipped.*

It was enough to make her head spin.

"I have her old journals," Leontina said quietly. "She left them with my old nanny, who you may recall Father chucked out when I was ten. He felt he'd already spent more than necessary on the care of a pointless female. That's a quote."

"I remember," Giaco said darkly.

"She wrote a lot about you," Leontina continued, still concentrating on the fingers in her lap. "Your gifts, your charms, the kind of man she thought you could be.

She loved you very much." She turned then and smiled at him, and that was far harder than it should have been. Because this wasn't new—she'd just never said it out loud to anyone before. "She didn't write that way about me. She hardly mentioned me at all."

This had always underscored what Umberto had told her, she'd always thought.

But Giaco did not nod solemnly, acknowledging at last what Leontina had known all along. What she expected him to finally admit, here and now, in the face of the proof she'd had all along.

Instead, he let out a short laugh. "Because she didn't have to," he retorted.

"But—"

Her brother held up a bruised hand. "I've thought a lot about this, particularly since I married Ivy. She's challenged me on a great many things that, I suppose, I took for granted. Our mother had learned to deeply fear men in her short time on this earth. She might have loved me, but I feel certain she was far more concerned that I might turn out to be the kind of man our father is."

He fixed that gaze of his on Leontina—the one that was so much like hers. Like their mother's, come to that. And when she didn't protest, he continued. "If it feels to you that she was giving you less attention, I'll point out to you that you're the one she left her words to. Not me. She *expected* you to be strong, like she was and then some. She wasn't *worried* about what sort of person you'd become, because look at you. You're the one who decamped in the night, leaving the old man reeling. If I'd managed that years ago, who knows who I'd be now?"

"I think," Leontina managed to say, "that you could only ever be you, Giaco."

He shook his head, something like a smile on his face. "How is it that you've managed to hide your true face—even from me—for all these years?"

"It's the same face." She looked at him, then looked back at the rows of weapons. Again, they seemed to be a part of this conversation. Because there were always all sorts of weapons at hand, in any situation. It only took some looking. "I just found that if you dress a certain way, and shuffle about, no one looks at your face. Not even your family."

"I have never pretended to be anything but a shallow creature," Giaco said after a moment, perhaps thinking about the times he, too, had not paid attention to his sister as she crept on by. "But it seems to me that you and I are two sides of the same coin, Leontina. I drew fire, because I thought it was keeping you safe. And you participated in that too, by keeping yourself safe by any means you could. Both of us did what was necessary to protect ourselves from that man according to her wishes, Leontina. Because, believe me, that's what she wanted."

Leontina felt herself trembling, as if something was erupting from deep within her. It felt as if her mother was closer than she'd ever been before, more *here* tonight than a half-imagined glimpse out of the corner of her eye.

She loved it so fiercely that she was terrified that if she tried to hold on to it this would all slip away. This moment. These revelations. An actual, adult conversation with Giaco at last. And if it all went back to how it was, then what would become of her?

There was no way she could handle it. Or allow it.

Beside her, Giaco shifted. "I hope you know that I was never going to let him sell you off to one of those idiots," he said then, in a fierce rush. "You didn't need to worry. Much less have what I presume were deeply salacious nights with a man who should have known better than to seduce an innocent, sheltered girl."

And Leontina wanted desperately to hold on to her mother. Because if she was to believe what Giaco was saying, and God knew she wanted to, her mother had been with her all along. If their mother hadn't *hated* her—and why had she believed her father in that when she knew what a liar he was?—but had simply expected her to carry on the mantle that she'd needed to set down, well. She could do that. She had done it.

But she couldn't allow Giaco's fantasy about what had happened between her and Pau to stand. Not only because he was wrong.

His being wrong didn't matter, really, but it was possible this might be her only opportunity to set the record straight. To tell someone the truth about what had happened. Maybe to unburden herself, sure. But maybe also because she needed to not keep it all inside her any longer.

And no matter what, on this night of truths, this one seemed crucial to share.

"He did not seduce me, Giaco," she said, as clearly and crisply as she could. "I seduced him."

When Giaco could not seem to control his face, and the skepticism that clearly took him over, she tilted her head to one side. Then she looked at him without a single shred of patience remaining.

"Excuse me. I am *your* sister, after all. Did you think you were the only Tavian capable of producing a few wiles at your convenience? You are not." She shook her head at him. "Just because *you* never saw my true face doesn't mean that no one else ever has."

She had the great satisfaction, then, of watching her brother take that on in real time. He did not accept it easily.

Good, she thought, thinking of Pau's bruised face.

And while he was processing the idea of his baby sister as a kind of femme fatale who could potentially match his energy in some way—something so delightful to contemplate that she thought she would have to return to that, later, for her own entertainment—she pushed on to the really critical bit of the whole thing.

"And the seduction was easy," she said. "As I'm sure you know. From your own voluminous experiences, of course."

Her brother winced. "I beg of you, do not feel the need to go into the details," Giaco muttered and raked his hands through his hair.

This, too, was validating—but she pushed on.

"What's a whole lot harder," Leontina continued, and she had to *order herself* to keep going, "since we're sitting here baring ourselves to the unflinching light of honesty on this historic night, is that I'm in love with him."

She laughed after she said it, because she'd never thought that she'd say such a thing out loud. It was exposing. It was terrifying. It might open her up to scorn, ridicule. Possibly worse things she hadn't imagined yet.

And also because it hurt. Because it all hurt.

She looked at her brother, almost helplessly. "It's terrible, Giaco, but there it is."

And for a moment, Giaco only stared at her. He looked something like alarmed.

Then, far more horrifying, he moved closer to put his arm around her and pulled her into another hug.

"I am so sorry," he said, and she heard no theatrics in his voice. No drama. He sounded sincere and it broke her heart in ways nothing else could have. "I can't tell you how much I wish that you did not love him. Because I must tell you, Pau loves nothing but his vines."

He pulled back, and studied Leontina's face, and clearly didn't like what he saw there, because he squeezed her shoulders again. "Leontina. I have known him since we were eighteen. He's the coldest man I have ever met, which brings me no end of delight because I take pleasure in poking holes in that chill. But I cannot think of anyone I would prefer you to love less, because he will not return those feelings easily."

Or at all, he did not say, and yet it seemed to hang between them anyway.

"Thank you for that," she managed to get out. "But I fear it's too late."

This time when she burst into tears, he let her cry on his shoulder. He rubbed her back. And it wasn't that it wasn't soothing or that she didn't love this new familiarity with the older brother she had always idolized.

But it didn't fix anything, either.

Particularly not her heart, because it had been beating for Pau alone for far longer than she wished to admit.

Even to herself.

CHAPTER EIGHT

WHEN PAU RETURNED to the dining room, he brought staff with him, and had them add a place setting the small table. He found the Tavian siblings standing together at the balcony, watching him too closely with matching sets of wary jade green eyes.

"I assume the two of you are no strangers to awkward family dinners," he said.

They only stared back at him and Pau was not one to wait upon permission anywhere—much less in his own house. He waved his hand at the table in some kind of invitation, then seated himself.

After moment, Giaco and Leontina followed.

He took this as the victory it was. Or, at the very least, as an improvement on letting his best friend punch him in the face.

"Now, at last, I feel at home," Giaco said with a big sigh and a matching smile when the silence stretched on too long. "There's nothing that excites me more than a heavily pregnant silence, unless it is a perfectly placed and diabolically subtle insult that lands four hours later, then keeps recipient up all night."

"Remind me when that was," Leontina murmured,

and aimed that smile of hers at her brother. "When you were subtle, I mean?"

Giaco laughed—genuinely this time—and Pau thought that perhaps it was all a bit lighter after that. A bit easier.

And whatever Leontina and her brother had spoken about when he was out of the room, the atmosphere seemed different between them, too. As if they'd finally found some common ground. Or a way to bridge the years that their father had certainly never fostered.

Not for the first time in his life, though for the first time in a long while, Pau wondered what it would have been like to have a sibling. To have someone else to share all of these experiences with, good and bad and everything between. His cousin had been around when he was younger, but not in the same way. And though he knew, of course, that there was a significant age differential between Leontina and Giaco, there was still also a shared sense of *who* they were.

They had both grown up in that castle. They had both lost their mother. They both still detested their father, openly.

They were Tavians.

He could not help but think it must make things easier, to carry such a load together.

In fact, he knew it did. Because all the things he'd done to prepare the chessboard to take down Umberto had been something he had done with Giaco. He hadn't been a lonely vigilante, out there chasing down the man responsible for his father's death, like every fantasist Hollywood loner film he'd ever accidentally seen.

The taking down of Umberto Tavian had been a

joint enterprise, and no wonder these last few months had felt so off. Pau might have been an only child. He might have felt a deep responsibility to this land and the family's legacy and the business too, but he hadn't been alone in this fight of his since way back when he was a teenager.

It made sense that this solo venture of his had made him feel so much like a stranger to himself. That notion seemed to kindle something deep inside him, a bright pop of something like self-incrimination—because it couldn't be anything else, he told himself sternly. It couldn't be the way he'd felt standing in that examination room, his hand held fast between Leontina's taut, rounded belly and her palm. The strange, rubbery, glorious sensation of his own child reaching out to him there—as if his son already knew him.

Just as it couldn't be the fact that, revenge or no revenge, he had found it remarkably difficult to keep Leontina out of his head since he'd first laid eyes on her in Italy. He'd studied her, looking for a way in, and had found contradictions and disguises. Then she had come to him, and he'd found a kind of communion he hadn't known existed—

But that was merely sex, he told himself harshly, and not something he needed to think about in the presence of his friend. Her brother. The architect of the current swelling on his face.

They ate. They talked of incidental things that caused no dark ripples. The grape harvest. How Giaco and Ivy were getting on with things now that the glare of the paparazzi was perhaps beginning to ebb. The connective tissue of their lives that could, Pau supposed, have a thousand reasons to intertwine that had nothing to do with the behavior of one old ogre of a man they all hated.

They talked of the health of the baby. Giaco advanced his choice of name for the child, which was, to no one's shock, Giaco.

When Leontina laughed at that—laughed and laughed, with no artifice in sight—Pau found that *popping* sensation inside him even more impossible to ignore. It was the careless joy on her face. It was the way she wiped at her eyes, but not because she was sad.

It made him think a bit too much about how little laughter there had ever been in this house. That, along with these family dinners that he found he liked even with his bruises tonight, had to become a staple of his child's life as it had not been of his. He did not wish to question himself on why that seemed of such critical importance to him now.

After dinner, when Leontina took a long look at the two men opposite her and then excused herself, Pau and Giaco sat there a moment. The sky above them was an inky black swirled through with too many stars to begin counting. The air smelled of fall, and of the winter to come. The staff had rolled the freestanding heaters closer to the table before they'd served the main course, and the temperature was pleasant.

Pau might not have known how to have a brother, so he did what he did know how to do. He prepared his friend's favorite drink at the bar inside, and then sat there with him in the weight of it all.

Giaco eyed him, but did not speak. An indictment

if ever there was one, to Pau's mind. For nothing was more concerning than Giaco Tavian *silent*.

Or, a tart voice within him suggested, sounding not unlike Leontina in one of her bolder moods, *perhaps you have a guilty conscience. As you should.*

"I should have told you what I was doing, Giaco," he said abruptly, though the words felt strange and acidic in his mouth. Likely because he had not apologized, to anyone, in longer than he could recall—and not because he believed himself a blameless, spotless human. But because he had long endeavored to live the kind of life that did not require an apology tour. "I should not have kept all of this a secret from you."

"Indeed you should not have," Giaco agreed, but he did not look *murderous*. This seemed like an upgrade from earlier in the evening.

"I don't think that I realized until now…" He shook his head. "I suspect you might not like it, but I thought that it was the family relationship, the fact that she is your sister, that would bother you. That your brotherly instincts would kick in and you would be angry about it, as brothers always seem to be."

"I know I have played the part of a man who feels nothing at all," Giaco said quietly. "But I assumed that you—perhaps only you, across a great many years—knew better."

Pau inclined his head. "I do know better. Yet it was not until tonight that I realized that this course of action was also, on some level, a betrayal of our partnership. And more, our friendship."

"You've known me a long time." Giaco swirled the amber liquid around in his tumbler, his bruised knuckles catching the lights. He had a curious look on his face. Pau didn't think he'd ever seen it before. "In that time, have I ever struck you as the sort of person, much less an older brother of a fully grown woman, who would become distraught about a bit of fucking?" He shook his head. "Please. What do you take me for?"

"That's my point." Pau shook his head. "The brotherly relationship baffles me. I would have assumed that nothing would bother you, but given that the point was to spring this as a fait accompli upon your father, secrecy had to be maintained. But the swelling of my eye suggests that I was wrong about that, does it not?"

Giaco gazed at him, then set his drink down. Decisively. "Pau. The only thing I care about is if my sister felt taken advantage of at any point in this." He lifted a brow. "Do you feel that she did?"

Pau felt his jaw tense. Because how could he answer that to Giaco's satisfaction? He had worried about precisely that and then it turned out that Leontina had been scheming all along. But how could he tell her brother such a thing if he didn't already know it?

If, on some level, he did not really know who his sister was?

He remembered too late that Giaco was sitting in front of him, watching him, and was not at all certain what expression he had on his face. He tried at once to modify it into something more impassive.

"She does not appear to believe I did," he said, carefully, and had to clear his throat. There seemed, suddenly, to be too many pressure points in too many places and he was not at all certain that he wasn't broadcasting them all. "I can only look back at my own behavior and take solace in that."

He thought he saw Giaco smile, though he hid it as he took a pull from his drink.

"In any case," his friend murmured, sounding significantly more pleased with himself than Pau thought he should tonight, "you must realize that I have always known that my father intended to sell Leontina off. It has long been one of his great, sick obsessions that he can create a mighty and impregnable dynasty by auctioning off his only daughter like some kind of raffle prize." Giaco lifted a shoulder, then dropped it, though the way he looked at Pau seemed almost... knowing. "Had you come to me and told me you wanted to marry her, whether because you thought that would be an excellent way to stick the knives in deeper into my father's back—and I agree with you, it's perfect— or whether you simply *liked* her, I would have had the same response. You have long been the finest man I've ever known, Pau. I would have been delighted to support you in this venture, had you only told me about it in advance."

"Thank you," Pau said dryly. "Speaking of sticking knives in."

This time, his friend did not try to hide his smile.

"In any case, it is done now," Giaco said. He waved a hand. "My sister is not unhappy, she informs me, and so I therefore have no complaint. And, of course, we know that you have never allowed a stray feeling to take purchase within you, so no worries that this will become any sort of emotional quagmire."

He lifted his glass, still smiling, though Pau found

that he was in no way reassured. And that, in fact, it felt as there were purchases aplenty within him that he could not have named if his life depended on it.

But Giaco was smiling at him, even more broadly now. "Now we are brothers in truth, old friend. That is our celebration."

That was what they did for the rest of that evening, though it was a far cry from the sort of celebration they might have had in their university years, or any of the sorts of celebrations Giaco was famous for. Not to mention those that had gotten him forcibly removed from many places. But it suited who they were now, Pau thought.

Though when he thought it, he wasn't sure he was quite ready to compare his marriage to his friend's. That seemed…dangerous.

They spoke of the plots they'd brought to fruition. They laughed about the brash proclamations they'd made when they were eighteen about the lives they would lead, and how pleased they were that most of them had not gone anywhere.

When they parted later that night, Pau had the staff lead Giaco to one of the guest suites, but not before they clapped each other on the back. And called each other *brother* yet again, meaning it perhaps more than they had before.

The moment Giaco disappeared, making the overly charmed staff member giggle as they went—because he might have been happily married but he was still Giaco Tavian, after all—the only thing Pau could think about was Leontina.

But that felt loaded tonight. His face ached from his

best friend's fists. He'd had to defend what had happened between him and Leontina when, deep down, he wasn't certain he should. Or even wanted to, because Leontina was his wife and they were having a son and what else should matter but that?

Especially when there were too many of those *pressure points* still, bearing down on him in ways he couldn't explain away. No matter how he tried.

Still, the fact that Giaco was under the same roof made Pau feel a lot as if this house was still a monastery. He thought he'd shower, see if he needed to put something cold on his face, and call it a night.

But when he went into his bedroom to change out of his clothes, he stopped dead, because she was there.

Leontina was in his bed, her dark hair spread out on the pillow and her eyes closed, looking like every fantasy he'd ever pretended he didn't have of her. She looked like a painting. Painfully perfect and bright—

And then she made it that much better when she opened her eyes as if she sensed him standing there at the foot of the bed.

"I was going to come find you," he said, though until that moment, he hadn't realized that he'd been lying to himself about *calling it a night*. That he could no longer imagine a night without her.

That he would have found her tonight no matter if Giaco was sleeping across her doorframe.

The smile she gave him then bore no resemblance to that false one she trotted out on social occasions, and it only became more precious to him the more he saw it. "I've been meaning to talk to you about this," she told him. "Why are we in different wings of this enormous, sprawling house? It's tedious, Pau. And soon enough, I will be entirely too large to be waddling all around, trying to find you every evening."

That simply, that easily, the whole night seemed to coalesce inside him. His lip was split still, and tender. He did not need to look in the mirror to know that his eye was likely blackening with every breath.

And yet, somewhere inside his chest, it was like he was someone new. Things between Giaco and him had been solved—despite his friend's *knowing looks* that he still could not entirely define—and that could only be a good thing. But it was a weight he hadn't entirely understood he was carrying, not really. Not until now, when it was gone.

And now there was Leontina. In his bed, where every last part of him seemed to shout that she belonged.

He didn't know why he was so determined to fight the very thing he'd wanted to happen. That he'd made happen. That he had envisioned being, perhaps, more distant than this—but why was he opposed to a marriage that, run probabilities though he did, he could only describe as significantly healthier than most of the other ones he'd ever witnessed?

Including his own parents' marriage, which had always seemed more businesslike to him than anything else, though not for his mother's lack of trying. After she had left him for her current life in Melbourne, Australia—where she assured her son, when she bothered to ring, that she was much-adored by her many lovers and did not care to ever return to Spain, where she had withered on the not-exactly-proverbial vine—Pau thought his father had been pleased.

No need to even *pretend* to care about anything but the vineyard.

He'd been barely ten when she'd left and he'd always vowed that should he marry, even if it was for purely business-related reasons, there would be no *withering*.

Yet here was Leontina, ripe with his child and in his bed, and he was standing about questioning…anything?

"I will inform the staff to move you in at once," he told her, perhaps more intently than necessary. He saw the answering heat in her green eyes. "After all, Leontina, we are husband and wife."

"Indeed we are," she agreed, her gaze grave. She sat up and he saw that she was wearing one of those silken little gowns that he'd discovered he quite enjoyed. Slinky little straps on the shoulder and then slippery silk everywhere else. Her belly looked tighter, rounder, tonight. Her hair tumbled down around her and the scent of it teased his senses.

Pau was convinced that he had seen no greater beauty in all his days.

"There is something I have to tell you, Pau," she said, and her gaze grew even more serious.

"That sounds rather dire," he pointed out. "I hope this conversation will come with fewer face punches. I believe I've had my fill for the evening."

"I don't know if it is dire or not," Leontina replied, sounding as if she was choosing her words with care. "Or rather, I have felt terribly guilty about this for months. I've wrestled with myself about whether or not to tell you at all. It could be that telling you is purely selfish. Yet part of me thinks that if I tell you, even if you find it difficult to forgive me right now, you will in time. Another part of me thinks that the sin was mine and so, too, should this be mine to live with."

"I think you had better tell me what it is," Pau said, though he suspected he knew. Because, as he had told her once already, he somewhat doubted that the girl who had saved herself for her brother's wedding, and had then spent that whole, long, transformative night in his arms the way she had, could then…wander off into a life of scandal and excess within a few months. Still. He already knew this woman, his wife, contained more multitudes than most. "Because the more you explain it without telling me, the more dire it seems."

Leontina blew out a breath. She folded her hands over her belly, and for a moment he thought he saw pure anguish in her eyes.

Pau found he hated it.

"My brother came here because he was convinced you'd somehow tricked me," she told him with great solemnity. "That you took advantage of my innocence and used it against me."

"I believe that most people will assume that's exactly what I did," he told her, though he could feel that pressure within him, seeming to *expand* as she gazed at him. "I am not sure that isn't a perfectly valid description of what happened."

"Well, it isn't. You didn't take advantage of me at all." She said that fiercely. Unapologetically, even. "I had every intention of seducing you that night, Pau. I'd read up on it."

"You'd *read up on it*?" he asked, doing his best not to

laugh. Then found that he was stunned that he *wanted* to laugh in the first place. It was as if the real price of this marriage was becoming the sort of man he'd never thought he was allowed to be. Not when there was so much work to be done and the family honor to uphold. But he shoved that aside. "Where did you read up on it, may I ask?"

"The internet is a font of information," she told him, frowning slightly. "With a great many illustrations. I knew that you'd attend the wedding. I read up on you, too. It was all part of my plan. I knew that my father was going to try to marry me off and I decided that I wanted to choose my own destiny."

"So perhaps more choices have been made than are immediately apparent," Pau said quietly.

He could see that she remembered that conversation, too. "That's what I'm trying to tell you. I did this. I created a package and I presented it to you, but I knew exactly where it would lead. That being, exactly where I wanted it to go."

And he could see that she meant this. With every part of herself, she meant it.

Pau could see that she was bracing herself for his reaction. A reaction she clearly expected to be volcanic.

He studied her for a long moment.

"I understand you may have to sit with this a while," she said, and he could see that she was being brave. She was holding herself so still. She was ready for him to explode—the way, he supposed, her father always had.

But he was certainly no Umberto Tavian.

"Leontina," he said, quietly, "I do not have to sit with

this. I do not have to search my soul to find ways that I might feel taken advantage of."

He moved then, shrugging out of his shirt and kicking off his trousers. Then he crawled onto the bed and made his way toward her like some kind of great predator in the wild.

And he had the pleasure of watching her eyes go wide.

"Do you have any idea just how many women tried their wiles on me at that wedding?" he asked her.

He could see she hadn't considered that. She blinked. "What do you mean?"

"I stopped counting," Pau told her. "I'm a very particular man, Leontina. And I don't do a single thing that I don't want to do. If I hadn't wanted you, there is no power on this earth that would have compelled me to take you to my bed. You do understand that, do you not?"

"I seduced you," she said again.

"My sweet girl, you did, but not in the way you mean." He didn't understand what was happening to him. It was as if he'd been taken over by…something. Some force outside himself, or perhaps those pressure points inside him had altered their shape. He couldn't name it, but it was as if the very bones of his chest had changed. As if they were holding his heart differently. He could not account for it, but he couldn't deny it, either. "It was my intention all along to seduce you, but I imagined it would be a necessary chore, nothing more. Surely you must realize by now, you are many things, but certainly no *chore*."

"A chore," she echoed. Then she laughed that marvelous laugh of hers that made his precarious chest ache. "Were we seducing each other, then?"

He thought that laugh would have done the trick on its own.

But he was closer now, and so he kept crawling until she was lying on her back. He came down beside her and half over her, so he could smooth a hand over her face and hold her cheek in his palm.

"I think we must have been seducing each other that night," he agreed. And then, so close to her, he smiled, and no matter that it felt strange on his face. "I could have put you out of your agony some time ago, I'm afraid. Because I knew you were trying to seduce me. It suited me."

She blinked. He wondered if she would take this badly—but instead, she smiled. "In that case, I have nothing to apologize for," she said, letting that smile work its magic all over him.

"Nothing at all," he agreed.

He remembered, so clearly, the notion he'd had that he would fuck the truth out of her, but this was different. It was more like he'd exposed the truth between them instead, and it was beautiful.

Their mouths met, and held. Everything seemed to come from those smiles they shared. Everything seemed bright and warm, like sunshine even though it was night.

His hands worshipped her. Her mouth astounded him. He smoothed his hand down that sweet silken gown, and didn't bother to tug it out of his way.

He found her wet and ready beneath her gown, without the hindrance of panties, and he sighed a little as he played with her silken folds and all that heat she generated. His cock was hard, so hard that he should have ached with need, and perhaps he did—but that, too, seemed a part of the golden sweetness of this.

Pau pulled her on top of him and lowered her slowly—very slowly—onto the head of his cock, then let her settle herself as she would until he was lodged deep inside. He slid his hands to the crease at the tops of her thighs and groaned out his appreciation as she began to rock herself against him.

Because he was mesmerized by her. Bewitched.

Besotted, something whispered inside him.

She moved on him like a dream. Like light. Like some kind of goddess, come to earth for reasons opaque and glorious and *bright*.

Leontina braced her hands on his abdomen as her hips moved slicker, faster. Together, they came closer and closer to that grand shimmering that he could feel already, waiting *just there*, beckoning them on.

Her hair fell around them like a curtain. He had a feeling of wholeness then, rushing through him and making him feel more grounded. More *here*. And more, he hadn't realized until now how very isolated he had always felt. Giaco had changed that, sure.

But now there was Leontina, and she'd blown it all up.

He couldn't imagine how he could ever do without her.

And when the crisis came, it was a wash of light. Golden, beautiful, sweeping them both up and washing them away, changing them forever.

Pau was certain that his heart had burst free of his own chest, and was hers now. Lost to him forever.

Something he might have found alarming if she wasn't so beautiful, smiling at him as if she was the only sun that mattered, lighting up the whole world.

And then she settled down against him with her mouth in his ear, panting and limp, and whispered three impossible words.

"I love you," Leontina said.

And ruined everything.

CHAPTER NINE

Leontina knew it was a mistake the moment she said it. A terrible mistake. It was as if he turned into a glacier beneath her.

He said nothing, but then, he didn't need to speak. She could feel the change in the room. In him. It was like someone had thrown open a window in the dead of winter to let the cold rush in.

She opened her mouth to take it back. To laugh, and claim it was the orgasm going to her head, making her speak nonsense like it was truth, making her silly and foolish and whatever else she had to say to make the glacial expression he wore thaw—

But she didn't.

She couldn't.

Leontina felt as if she'd been waiting the whole of her life to say these things to him. As if the point of her life was not only to say what she'd said, but to *feel* it.

And she did feel it. She felt it everywhere, from the tiniest bones in her feet to the heart that was beating too hard in her chest. It didn't matter that she knew he wouldn't receive her love well. Giaco hadn't needed to warn her—she'd already understood the situation she was in.

She didn't have to have experience with half the world to read Pau. She had experience with him. Their relationship might not have been long, but it had been intense. On both sides of those three months.

Yet Leontina could not have kept those words inside if her life depended on it.

The girl who'd hidden all her life to avoid her father's various schemes and rages, tantrums and vile friends, could not hide here. Not in his man's arms. Not when they were too many things to each other already. Not when they would only become more entwined as this went on, this nine-month shift from a wild night to parenthood.

She tried her best to force the words out anyway, any words that might fix this, but she couldn't.

Pau set her aside as he shifted, then rolled to the edge of the bed. She thought for a moment that he might sit there the way he had the other night. She remembered how lonely he'd looked, and wondered if things would have been different now if she'd reached out then. If she might have built some kind of bridge there that would help her now.

He didn't stay at the edge of the bed tonight. Pau barely paused. Instead, he stood immediately and stalked off to the bathroom.

She wanted to follow him. She was afraid to follow him.

But Leontina also couldn't allow fear to dictate to her, not in this new iteration of her life. Not when she would shortly have to teach a child a better way to grow up than what she'd suffered through. Not when she had gone to the trouble to escape the life her father wanted for her.

So she forced herself to get up. To follow him into the bathroom on bare feet, and watch him as he splashed water on his face, then patted himself dry with a towel, all while going out of his way to keep from looking at her.

As if the very sight of her might *wound* him, somehow.

"You don't have to say it back," she said quietly. "I didn't ask anything of you. I only told you how I felt. You could as easily have ignored it."

Though she could not imagine that would have felt much better.

"I will not discuss this, Leontina," he said, coldly. Still avoiding her gaze. He stalked to the lustrously tiled shower and turned on the hot water, so hot and immediately steamy that she considered warning him that he risked melting off his ice-cold exterior that way.

But somehow she doubted he would find that amusing.

"Pau—"

His dark eyes slammed into her, ringed with gold and shot through with what looked to her like outrage and pure betrayal. "If you love me, I advise you to listen to me," he bit out. "I suggest you get some sleep. Your brother will be here in the morning and I expect he will provide enough emotion to go around."

"Do you think he'll take a swing at you again?"

"He will not." Pau's voice was as dark as his gaze now, and she could hear the betrayal in that, too. "I earned what happened tonight. But that will be the end of me simply sitting back and taking blows. I feel certain he knows this."

"I'm sorry he hit you," Leontina said quietly. "I would have hit him for you, but I doubted that would do much besides annoy him."

"I do not require my wife and the mother of my child to engage in fisticuffs on my behalf, thank you," Pau said icily. The words *wife* and *mother* had made her feel so connected to him before. It was a sad little marvel that he could use them now to create distance.

Gulfs upon gulfs of distance.

He stalked into the shower, and Leontina debated whether or not she should follow him in there. It was one thing for him to walk off out here, but there was nowhere to go in that stall. It was large and steamy and they had spent a great deal of time in there over the past weeks.

She found herself hesitating, and shook herself.

If she loved this man, surely that meant she didn't have to contort herself around his moods or parse the look in his eyes for clues on how to act. If she loved him that had to mean that she needed to behave in the exact opposite fashion than she would if she was back at the castle, where *love* was not a word she'd ever heard used. By anyone.

A life she would not accept for her son, but that was getting ahead of herself.

The question was, would she meekly wait for him like she was waiting out a storm? Or was she finished with that part of her life? If she had to take cover from the man she loved, she needed to do something about her heart's terrible choices.

Leontina hoped she'd learned at least that much.

She blew out a breath, then followed him into the shower.

The steam billowed, but it wasn't enough to disguise the glory that was Pau, naked, as he stood with his arms braced against the wall and let the stream of water pound into his back.

"I will not discuss it," he gritted out as she came in and let the water wash over her. She slicked her hair back from her face and decided that now was not the time to start a discussion about unilateral decrees in a marriage, which she did not recall agreeing to in that deeply civilized discussion they'd had when they'd decided to marry.

So calm. So quiet.

And she felt nothing like that now.

"Then let's not discuss it," she replied, and that made him turn from the shower wall, a frown all over his face.

"Leontina—" he began.

But this time *she* was the one not having the discussion.

Instead, she moved closer, and then sank down to her knees before him. The water fell all over them, adding a different dimension to this act that he had taught her that first night. Oh, she'd read about it. She'd studied the pictures she'd found and had watched some videos online that she rather wished she hadn't. She'd thought she had the general idea.

Pau had tutored her in the reality of it. He'd taken

such care then. He'd guided her head, murmured his approval, told her she was beautiful—though he hadn't finished in her mouth.

Tonight he would, she vowed.

If she couldn't have his love tonight, she would have the taste of him instead.

She swayed forward and slid her hands along his hair-roughened thighs, and could feel something like an electric current beneath his skin, making him *almost* seem to shake. She knelt up, and could see his hands at his sides, curling into fists.

But he didn't set her away from him.

And by the time she got to his cock, it was jutting out proudly, hard and ready.

Making his determination to get away from her... silly, really.

Leontina did not need to belabor the point. It was already made. She wrapped both of her hands around his cock, one at the base and the next right on top of it, leaving her ample real estate to play with. She gripped him, then tilted her head back to find his gaze.

His dark eyes were glittering. Ferocious. His nostrils flared as he looked down the length of his own body to her kneeling there at his feet.

She kept her gaze fixed on him as she leaned forward and licked the tip of him, smiling when she felt a shudder go through him and the pulse she could feel in her hands kick into a higher gear.

Then she swirled her tongue around the thick head, like he was an ice cream cone, and sucked him into her mouth.

And then she did as she pleased.

She tasted him. She played with him. She moved her hands up and down his shaft as she worked the head, and was rewarded for this by the way he groaned and began to move his hips to meet her.

His hands ended up in her hair, guiding her as he slowly began to increase the speed of his thrusts. She could watch him as she did this, as she took what she wanted from him and gave him so much pleasure in return. Pau had his back against the slick shower wall, his head thrown back, and a look of such powerful intensity on his face that she could feel it between her own thighs.

In fact, the wilder his thrusts got, the more she felt it in her core, as if he was licking her himself.

And when he finally stiffened, then shouted out her name, he pumped himself into her mouth. Everything was salt and heat, and she drank him down greedily.

Then kissed him there, on that broad head, as she pulled away.

For a moment, they stayed like that. The water fell all over them. It made her hair seem darker, there against her skin. He was still holding a hand to her head, as if he hadn't thought to let it drop. Or couldn't quite make himself let go.

He still stood with his head thrown back, leaning against the wall. And Leontina found that watching this man when he couldn't see her felt like a gift. He looked so much more approachable like this, sated and close, the bold lines of his face softer than when his eyes were open.

She remembered that night in the castle, when they'd both passed out after one of their wild, intense rounds and she'd woken up first. Maybe that was the first inkling she'd had that this was not going to be as simple or straightforward as she'd imagined it would be. As she'd told herself it would be.

After all, he was Pau Calixto. He was—famously—no monster. And Leontina had always known that a love match for her was unlikely. If her father got his way, she would have been sold off to the highest bidder—not exactly a recipe for tenderness.

She had studied the guest list for the wedding obsessively and had settled on Pau almost immediately. It had been a bonus that he was the potential partner her father had most wanted to impress, but she would have chosen him anyway. She had known he wouldn't hurt her the way the men her farther chose for her would. She had known he was admired for his moral compass and considered a good man among too many sharks.

If a girl had to marry a stranger, she'd thought that night, she could do a lot worse than finding a way to make that stranger be this one.

But now, here in this hot, steamy shower with the taste of him on her tongue, she wondered if the truth was that she'd fallen in love with him there and then.

His hand dropped from her head and she missed it immediately. He straightened from the wall and his eyes opened, then zeroed in on her at once.

And if she was expecting to see some kind of softening there, some kind of hope, she was sorely mistaken.

He looked more fiercely forbidding than he ever had.

"Pau," she began.

He only shook his head, something deeply ferocious

in the gesture, and stalked from the shower, leaving her there.

For a long while, Leontina wasn't sure that she could breathe.

She didn't hear his footsteps as he left the bathroom and the suite beyond, but she knew he was gone.

Eventually, she got to her feet. She turned off the water and got out of the shower, then took her time toweling herself dry. Maybe she was pretending that if she went back into the bedroom, he would be there waiting—but she knew he wouldn't be. He wasn't.

She stood there, her feet on the stone floor, the moonlight dancing its way through the windows, and her heart like a cement block in her chest.

It was almost worse that she knew, deep down, that he hadn't left the estate. He likely hadn't left the house. Pau was far too conscious of his responsibilities for that. He just didn't want to be near *her*.

Leontina thought she ought to react to this more dramatically, to match the wild mess inside her. Sob and scream, perhaps. Fling herself onto the floor, and salt the stone with her tears. Maybe rend her own nightgown, tear her hair, and any other expression of grief she could come up with.

But she did none of those things. She turned to the bed instead, climbed into it, and pulled the covers around her. Then she curled up into a ball, hugging her belly close.

And for a long while, that was all she did. She breathed. She hugged herself. She let her mind spin out where it would.

But eventually, as she lay there, she started thinking about love.

Starting with her mother.

There had been something deeply healing in the conversation she'd had with Giaco earlier that night. It was as if he'd reached deep inside her and rearranged her bones—that was how catastrophically wonderful it had been. It was as if he'd made her new.

And it allowed her to think more critically about her childhood. About the lies her father had told her. All the things she'd believed about her mother and her death because he'd wanted her to believe them. Because it suited him, the sick and sadistic man that he was, to know that his daughter truly believed that she had essentially killed her own mother.

That she had been such a trial that her mother had seen no other way out.

Now it was like a boulder had been rolled away from that part of her heart. She felt nothing for her mother but sympathy. A deep sorrow. And after twenty-four years of Umberto's company, understanding as to why she'd had to do what she'd done.

But she also knew—with a deep comprehension that seemed more like something primal within her—that *she* could not make the same choice. Not ever.

She thought about Pau's shift into such coldness that she wasn't entirely certain she didn't have frostbite, no matter what had happened in that shower. The idea of a lifetime like that with him, stretching before her, was daunting.

They had agreed they would not divorce. They had talked about legacies.

He had been calm and distant then, but nothing like this. That had been a cool, refreshing breeze after a lifetime of Umberto's rages. Tonight had been an ice storm, and she wasn't sure she'd ever finish shivering. She was half afraid to check her own body, sure she'd find signs of hypothermia.

A lifetime in this kind of arctic chill could make all kinds of escape plans seem reasonable.

But she hugged herself tight as she lay there. She felt her baby kick in her belly, and it made her smile, and she knew with a bedrock certainty that she could never make the same choice her mother had.

That somehow, she would find a way to be neither diminished nor destroyed by this marriage. And that no matter how she felt about it, she would love her child more. Too much to ever leave by choice.

Maybe this was the strength that her mother had indicated to Giaco that Leontina had. Maybe it was a fierceness that her mother had lacked. Maybe the reason her mother hadn't written about her was that she knew that she was leaving behind a daughter who would have to do better, or be crushed.

All things were possible, Leontina thought. She felt grateful for her mother and sorry she hadn't known her better, the way her brother had.

"But I swear to you," she whispered to the baby inside her, smoothing her hand over the little foot that kicked at her, "I promise you, as long as I live, I will love you so much that if thousands of vicious men like Umberto claimed that I didn't love you, you would never believe them. They will never get purchase on your heart. *I promise.*"

When her son kicked inside her again, she felt as if they come to an agreement.

She closed her eyes then and thought instead of Pau. The man she loved.

Despite the fact that he was clearly suffering from some heretofore unknown head wound—because there could be no other explanation, surely, for him to react the way he had. Leontina was many things. Foolish, perhaps, in imagining that she in all her brash innocence could truly seduce a man like Pau, who had obviously been around every block there was to go around. No doubt a time or two. Or more.

But she thought that was the difference between book smart and street smart. Or sheet smart as the case might be in this situation. He'd had a lot to teach her in bed. She couldn't deny that.

Yet when it came to emotions, she thought that Pau was actually the virgin here.

She thought of what her brother had told her—that Pau loved only his vines and his legacy, and nothing else.

But Giaco had never been all that great at emotion himself. Leontina knew this not only because of her brother's much-publicized bad behavior all over the world's sparkliest places, but because she had seen the difference in him now that he was with Ivy.

Leontina had never dared try to get close to her stepsister while Ivy had still lived in the castle. It had been too dangerous. Umberto viewed all hints of closeness as ammunition. As weakness. She'd followed Ivy's life after she'd escaped the castle, so she knew the person her brother had married. Giaco was in no way the man he'd been before her.

The contrast was so profound that it could only be love.

She thought that in this case, having studied love more than either of them, she was the authority on this. She'd seen the look on his face when they'd been in his cousin's clinic. She'd heard what his cousin said—that Pau was a changed man. She'd seen the look on his face tonight.

So as she lay there in the fetal position, cradling her baby, she asked herself what she would think of her dynamic with Pau if she wasn't personally involved.

It wasn't hard to reach a conclusion.

In Leontina's expert opinion, her husband was completely in love with her, but terrified to admit that to himself. Much less to her.

She sat with that, waiting to see if it felt like maybe she was being a bit delusional. Or straight-up self-serving. Because, of course, that was what she would prefer the truth to be. She was in love with him already, so, of course, she'd love it if they matched.

But even if she *was* being delusional, she also knew that she had already survived an entire lifetime in the presence of a man who didn't love her at all. It was not ideal. It was not something she intended to subject her child to.

Though, with all her experience, it was certainly something she could survive until she made a new plan to escape.

And that notion was what almost made her cry.

She didn't *want* to escape. She really did love Pau.

Tonight it had seemed that she really had found her way home—to him—at last.

Leontina let her eyes go damp and let the pillowcase catch her tears as they fell. She did nothing to stop them.

She stayed where she was, curled in a damp ball, until morning.

"Both of you look a bit the worse for wear," Giaco said, because of course he did, when he sauntered into breakfast some thirty minutes after the staff had ushered Leontina in, so that she and Pau could sit there in the chilly silence.

She had considered pretending to be chirpy and happy to see her husband and to pretend that nothing had had happened last night, but she didn't. Because maybe it felt better to obey his unspoken demand—today, anyway—that she not attempt to talk to him.

Especially because the longer the silence drew out between them, the more tense that jaw of his became.

Giaco either didn't notice, or did notice and didn't care. He threw himself into his seat, helped himself to a generous pour of the blackest coffee, and beamed around the table. "I can only hope that you were up half the night, performing acts so salacious and degrading that you are hungover from them today. Yes, even you, Leontina. You are a pregnant, married woman who can have no claim to pearl clutching, surely."

Pau looked as if he might possibly have died inside, though his expression did not change.

"Good morning, Giaco," Leontina said, with a smile. "I understand that you take great pleasure—or did, certainly—in spreading your exploits hither and yon like some kind of sport But I do not."

To her surprise, her brother actually blinked. "Of course you don't," he said, in a voice that was very nearly *chastened*. "My apologies. Sometimes I forget myself."

"Sometimes we all do," Leontina said, though she glanced over at Pau while she said it. It was a pointless enterprise, since Pau was apparently pretending to be made of stone today.

But she could remember too clearly how it had tasted when he'd lost himself in her mouth, no matter how much strong *torrefacto* coffee she let herself sip.

After breakfast, she and Pau took Giaco on a tour of the vineyards. It was beautiful, as always, but for Leontina it was an opportunity to listen to Pau talk with great animation about this thing he did here. These ancient vines and the land they were a part of. All these things that made him who he was.

The things he actually loved.

She could almost convince herself that he *wanted* to melt.

That all she had to do was find a way to heat him up.

But when the tour was done, Pau went and locked himself up in the office with her brother for what she was pretty sure was a business conversation. Though for all she knew, they could have been planning new revenge schemes.

Afterward, Giaco took his leave—with another big hug that had her teary-eyed again—and then left Leontina and Pau alone again.

Or rather, as alone as anyone could be in the middle of a busy vineyard.

She didn't see Pau again until the evening, when she was quite surprised to find herself summoned to dinner.

"I was certain I'd been relegated to a tray on my own," she said to the maid, who looked horrified.

"No, madam," she stammered. "The master was very clear that you are to join him."

"I am honored," Leontina replied, and had to fight not to sound acerbic.

She took her time dressing, more because it made her feel as if she was wearing armor than because she thought it would have any specific effect on him. The house was as sprawled out as ever and so she took her time finding yet another little corner of the place that Pau could make into a dining room for an evening.

When she found it, she swept in, and then paused when she found him waiting at the windows, his back to her.

They had been in this dining room before, she realized belatedly. Then she wondered if they would continue to cycle through dining areas forever—but that wasn't how she greeted him. He wasn't in a space to entertain her questions, always meandering and with a thousand tangents.

That was what happened when a person's education involved wandering around a library at will and following rabbit holes wherever they might lead on the internet.

But tonight she looked at that cold, hard line of his spine and arranged her face appropriately. "I was so surprised to receive an invitation to dine with you, Pau.

After last night, I was certain you were going to avoid me for weeks."

"I believe we've had enough childishness in this marriage already," he said in that same arctic tone. She didn't like it any better tonight.

And that was clearly meant to be a dig, Leontina knew. She didn't take it as one, because she refused to accept that love had anything to do with childishness. He only wanted her to think so. Because it suited him for her to think so.

Because this man's reaction to his feelings was to turn them into vengeance.

It bothered her that she still didn't know why.

She might have some guesses—since she knew a thing or two about unavailable fathers—but she didn't *know*. He hadn't told her.

Today she had to wonder if he ever would.

She didn't react. She also didn't take her seat at the table. They stood there, on opposite sides of the room, as if they were facing off. Leontina let her hand rest on her belly and tracked the way his gaze followed the gesture, then jerked away.

As if he didn't want to think too closely about their child. Not when he was so busy impersonating granite.

"There's an attraction between us," he said after a moment, and Leontina was quite certain she wasn't imagining the patronizing note in his voice. It set her teeth on edge, but she didn't let herself outwardly react. She suspected that was what he wanted. "I imagine that surprised us both."

He said that last part as if he was being magnanimous. Leontina laughed.

"It didn't surprise me," she said, shaking her head at him. "Because I knew what you looked like. I suspect you were the one who was a little more surprised."

He didn't like that. She could see that all over his face. But he nodded. "That's likely true. Nonetheless, our connection has proven to be far more volatile than anticipated."

"Is that another way of saying that you had no intention of ever permitting yourself to have a single feeling where I was concerned?" she asked, perhaps too cheerfully.

Because she could see that her cheerfulness bothered him—and she might not think that it was fair to call anything that was happening here *childishness*, but she was only human.

She studied that absurdly perfect face of his and she could see the tightness of his jaw. The flatness of his lips. And that darkness in his gaze.

It made her wonder if he even knew what he felt about anything.

Though it was certainly not *cheerful*.

"I was trying to protect you," he said shortly. "But you've indicated protection is unnecessary. After all, you were under the impression that *you* seduced *me*." His gaze seemed darker. "The truth is, Leontina, this has nothing to do with you. It's what you represent. You are your father's last remaining hope to reclaim his standing in the nasty little worlds he inhabits. But I wanted to make sure that he has as little hope as he gave my father in the end."

Suddenly, Leontina felt significantly less cheerful.

"What do you mean?" she asked. "What did Umberto do to your father?"

Pau made a bitter sound. "He befriended him. At Giaco's wedding, I saw that your father has his own vineyard now. That's a new enterprise, isn't it? Ten years old or so, I would bet."

"I believe there were vines there before," Leontina said, though she felt a sense of foreboding. "But no one cultivated them. Not before I was around fourteen or so. That was when they got more serious."

"I don't know if you know this," Pau said, and he was still standing so straight, so tall, there by the window. Everything about him was dark and forbidding, and she knew this was about feelings because beneath it all, she could see that he was furious. "One of the things your father loves to do is find new ways to damage new people. After all, ruining the same people over and over is only so much fun. When he decided to start cultivating his wine, he naturally thought that he ought to branch out by connecting with established vintners. They were an exclusive group. Two in California, two in France, one in New Zealand, and my father here in Spain." His mouth took on a bitter curve. "Not one of them is in business any longer. And my father is dead."

Leontina stared back at him, trying to patch that together with the sense of foreboding she felt. "What exactly are you saying?"

Pau's dark eyes flashed. "My father thought he found a friend, and he loved nothing more than to talk at length about the one and only topic that interested him. While my mother was here, she liked to complain about his one-track mind. I think everybody found him too much, but it was who he was."

He paused then, and it seemed to hurt him to swallow. His eyes were even darker. Leontina found herself wondering if Pàu might have been the only one who didn't find Bernat Calixto to be *too much*—and that made her heart clench.

Yet Pau pushed on. "So when he found a friend who couldn't hear enough about his vines, his varietals, his soil composition, he had no barriers. No sense of self-preservation. He told your father everything he could possibly want to know, and in so doing, my father destroyed himself."

His eyes seemed to glow then, with the kind of temper Leontina had never seen on him before. "Because, naturally, your father did not want a friend. Your father has never had a friend in his life. He wanted information. And he took it. Every single one of the men he reached out to either died from the stress or went bankrupt, while your father's new enterprise did quite well because of them. Imagine that."

"I can imagine that quite well," Leontina said with a certain quiet fury of her own, because she hated this story. And not only because she hated that her father had gotten his talons into Pau's family, too. "That's what he does. That's who he is. I'm so sorry, Pau, that your father got caught in his crossfire."

"I appreciate that, Leontina, yet I don't find *sorry* to be enough," Pau hurled back at her. "My father loved only one thing. And your father took it from him. My mother beat her head against that wall for as long as she could. Part of me thinks that when she finally left, it was out of exhaustion. She was just so *tired* of trying to be the focus of my father's attention and never getting there." He shook his head. "And when I tell you that he never loved me either, I'm not looking for sympathy. It is simply the truth. And I can accept that, because I knew how much this land and our legacy meant to him." His dark eyes seemed to burn straight into her. "What I cannot accept is your father knew too, and took it from him anyway."

"My father is a terrible person," Leontina said, and perhaps she sounded a little impatient. "But this is well known. This is who he is. My question for you, Pau, is what do *you* love?"

"I loved my father," he bit out, and it was shattering.

She thought she would have preferred it if he'd hauled off and slapped her instead. It was that shocking.

That intense.

Because somehow, he sounded as arctic as before, and all she could think of was a little boy like the one she carried inside her own body. A little boy with dark eyes looking up to a man who did not possess the capability of returning that emotion.

So what could Pau possibly imagine except that love was unrequited, and then nothing but loss and grief?

It was heartbreaking.

At least Leontina had been lucky enough to have her brother. Whether they were close or not didn't matter. His very existence had helped her get over that helpless parental love early on, because Giaco was so bright and irrepressible and Umberto had hated him, too.

Once she'd understood that hate was all her father did, all he was capable of, she found ways to get healthier. She loved her books. She loved her escape fantasies. And sad though that might have been, it was better than this.

"Of course you loved him," she said quietly. "You are nothing if not dutiful, no matter what you get in return."

He didn't like that. She could see it all over his face like a kind of anguish, but he slashed his hand through the air as if he was casting that aside. Maybe her, too.

"You are my final act of revenge, Leontina," he told her coldly. So coldly, though his eyes were that dark gold, and they were bright now. "Because that is how I will honor my father's memory. Your father nearly took the only thing my father loved from him. It came so close that I believe it killed him. Struck him down where he stood. I can only hope that learning that I have returned that favor will do the same for Umberto."

"It will anger him," Leontina said. "But surely you must realize by now that my father does not feel anything. Ever."

"If it angers him, all the better," Pau growled.

"But—" she began.

"We leave tomorrow," he told her. When she only stared back at him without comprehension, his gaze darkened even more, like a new, worse storm coming in. "I'm taking you back to the castle."

CHAPTER TEN

LEONTINA WAS SUBDUED the next day, but Pau expected that.

What he had not anticipated was that he would feel something less than stellar himself, which made no sense, since he was finally enacting the final piece of his revenge against the loathsome Umberto Tavian. His plans had all come together, even better than he'd imagined they could. Today was a day of celebration.

Yet he somehow did not feel much like celebrating at all.

He should have been bursting with joy today, yet he felt…as close to *muddled* as he thought he'd ever been. As if all of that pressure inside him had *exploded* and left him reeling, when he prided himself on always being sharp and in command—and therefore, he had always hoped, immune to the sort of thing that had taken down his father. Pau did not intend to trust the wrong person, and usually he could depend on his tried-and-true discernment to make certain he was protected.

But there appeared to be no protection from Leontina and the things she made him feel—little as he wished to admit he felt anything at all—

The trouble was, he hadn't slept well.

After what had happened the night before, he hadn't told the staff to move Leontina into his room the way he'd said he would. He'd considered that the smart and only reasonable course of action, particularly after Leontina had responded to the news of their journey today by turning on her heel and leaving the dining room. Without a word.

But this meant, of course, that she hadn't been in his bed when he'd finally retired, after spending entirely too long scowling at the stacks of books in every corner of this house, noting which ones she'd taken out and looked at. After hours of wondering what, exactly, she'd learned about him in reading what he'd read, the way she'd said she would.

If he was the man he'd always thought he was, he'd kept thinking—for reasons that remained opaque to him even now—he would welcome this little project of hers. He would have nothing to hide.

That had been what had forced him to take himself off to bed. Because, of course, what *could* he have to hide? He was Pau Calixto. His life was a wide-open book, available to any who looked his way because he was precisely who he appeared to be, and the actual books in his home could only support that. And why should it matter to him what Leontina thought of him, anyway? They had decided to marry, and stay married, no matter what. The die was cast.

But he'd found himself standing in the center of his bedroom without any lights on, entirely too aware that she was not there.

As if her absence was a hole inside him.

When he'd finally thrown himself into the bed, he'd faced a very long night. Because the bed that had always seemed appropriately sized for him seemed entirely too big and empty without her.

He did not wish to contemplate how that was possible.

But even a long, hot shower had not helped, likely because Pau found that even the damned shower stall was no longer his. The entire monastery was haunted, not by the ghosts of his ancestors as might be expected, but by Leontina. He swore he caught her scent around every corner, only to turn it and find no one there.

He spent the morning furious that on this, his day of victory, he was unable to think of anything but her. And not because she was the means to his long-planned end, which would have been acceptable. He didn't know what it was, this dark obsession.

Pau only knew it plagued him.

When she appeared in the front hall at the appointed time, it was like a body blow. He hated that, too. She gazed at him with a guarded sort of calm that he found offensive, especially when her eyes were still too green, too dark, too compelling.

Maybe the real trouble was he remembered the night in the shower too vividly. Leontina on her knees in all of that steam, her jade gaze hot and fixed to his with his cock thrusting in and out of her perfect mouth—

She is a witch, he assured himself.

More importantly, this was not the day for such reminiscences. Today was about Bernat. It was about coming full circle. About Umberto, at last, reaping what he sowed.

"When you are ready," he intoned, and he was certain that there was something too knowing in the way Leontina looked at him. He was sure that she would speak up, because that was what she did—

But she didn't. She only inclined her head like the subservient wife she'd never been here, and somehow that was worse.

He found himself fuming as he ushered her out into the drive and saw her into the waiting vehicle. They sat in the back seat of the SUV as his men took them to the waiting plane, tucked away on his private airstrip. Yet somehow, though he could have reached out a hand and touched her at any point, he felt as if she was much farther away.

His tragedy was that he was far too aware of her just the same.

Pau had not given Leontina any directives about how she ought to dress for the occasion of returning to the home she'd escaped, but he could find no fault with the outfit she had picked. It was not one of her baggy dresses, which he hadn't seen at all in a long time. Today she'd chosen a long-sleeved dress in a dark hue that managed to emphasize her pregnant belly without clinging too closely anywhere else, making her look elegant and untouchable—especially with the jewelry she wore, hints of gold at her wrists, her ears, her neck. She'd twisted her hair back into a smooth ponytail, and it called attention to her classic, gorgeous features.

She bore no resemblance at all to the invisible girl in saggy clothes who crept about in the servants' stairs. She was, with no guidance from Pau at all, exactly who he wished to present to Umberto today.

So there was no reason at all that she should get under his skin.

Though he had a whole plane ride to think about it.

It was how at ease she seemed. How relaxed. She sat across from him on the plane and acted as if she was alone, and utterly unbothered, while he thought seriously about climbing the walls.

Landing in Tuscany did not make it any better. He felt almost…edgy, being back here. They moved from the plane to sit in the back of yet another vehicle, and this time, he tried to keep his gaze on the landscape. The cypress trees rose like taunts on every rolling hill.

And as soon as he saw Umberto's absurd castle heave into view, he felt restlessness all over him.

Pau told himself that this was foolishness. He had finally achieved what he wanted. He should have been filled with nothing but triumph. Perhaps he needed to actually parade Umberto's daughter in front of him and behold the old man's reaction to get the full effect.

Maybe he was expecting to feel all that triumph too early.

That said, he wasn't a complete fool. He had brought his security detail with him on this trip, because he didn't trust Umberto as far as he could throw him—and given that he would not touch the man if his life depended on it, that was not far. But Umberto could teach slithering to snakes. There was every reason to think the old man might well react violently once he realized he was truly backed into a corner.

Once he understood that Pau had bested him—again—and better yet, with the daughter Umberto had dismissed as unimportant except as a bargaining chip.

As the Land Rover navigated its way over ancient hills and winding roads, Pau could admit to himself that he rather hoped that the old man *did* try to get violent. His face already hurt from Giaco's fists. Why not fight *every* male in the Tavian family this week?

It would solve all manner of problems if Umberto tried, because unlike with Giaco, Pau would happily fight back this time. And he had no doubt that he would win.

How satisfying, he thought. It would tie things up neatly and truly bring it all full circle. It would be fitting in every way.

The only trouble was, he wanted Umberto to live a while with the knowledge he'd been bested.

Pau found himself regretting the fact that he was not more pugilistic. He allowed himself a few brief daydreams as the vehicle bumped along, but he preferred strategies and probabilities to wrestling matches. And he was so busy thinking about the various ways he would celebrate his enemy's death when the glorious day finally arrived that they were walking up to the grand front door of the castle itself before he realized that his wife had not spoken a word all morning.

He hadn't noticed because she had been like a thorn in his side all this while. The scent of her was driving him mad—he'd resorted to imagining himself some kind of cinematic action hero in defense.

"I doubt we will stay long," he told her, perhaps a bit more darkly than necessary, as they walked.

She looked at him then with that fake smile he detested welded into place and no hint of the Leontina he thought he knew in those dark jade eyes. Darker than usual, he thought. And far blanker. "As you wish, husband," she said.

So demurely it made him frown at her, and he was sure he saw an answering flare of the heat he knew—

But the castle doors were opening. And the staff took one look at Leontina, got wide-eyed, and ushered them both inside with his security detail at his heels.

"Welcome home," one of the staff murmured to Leontina, though the look on her face was more...*concerned* than welcoming.

The smile Leontina gave the woman was not fake. "I am not returning, I assure you," she said quietly. "Only visiting."

Pau thought the other woman looked relieved.

He found he was clenching his teeth, though this time it was because it was only occurring to him that he'd come up with this plan of his when he hadn't known Leontina. He'd decided exactly how it would end, but he'd made these decisions before he'd met her. Before he'd held her. Before she'd told him the stories of how she'd lived here for so long.

Before she'd begun to matter to him in ways he wasn't sure he knew how to articulate, even to himself.

That he hadn't thought to consider how *she* might feel about having to return here at all, much less to be paraded in front of her nasty father like the spoils of war—well.

Perhaps Pau had more in common with the father his mother had left than he cared to admit.

It was a long march through the old building, winding this way and that. Leontina was wearing absurdly high heels, though they did not seem to slow her down any. They clicked against the marble and stone impressively as she walked, somehow adding to her mystique in ways he felt take shape inside him. Though he wasn't sure he could name them.

Possibly because the only name in his head was hers.

All Pau knew was that his hunger for her had never been higher. Maybe it was because they were back here in this castle and the last time they had been here, they'd spent an epic night together. More than simply enjoying each other, repeatedly, they had created their son.

It was difficult not to look back and consider that night magical now.

He just wished she hadn't said those words. He would have done anything to rewind time, to keep her from saying them out loud.

Even if it meant it took longer to reach this stage in his end game.

That thought hit him like another unexpected hook to the mouth. Since when had he ever—*ever*—let anything come between him and his revenge? Even hypothetically?

But they had arrived at a set of ostentatious doors where a man dressed entirely in unctuous black stood.

"The master waits within," the man said, deferentially, and bowed.

Then he stood and turned crisply, throwing open the two doors at once in what was, clearly, a piece of deliberate choreography.

"Enter, please, the chamber of *Umberto Tavian* himself," the man in black intoned, like he was auditioning for town crier.

But the bland look Leontina sent him made Pau think

that all of this was a bit of theater for an audience of one. And not an unusual occurrence.

He took that as a good sign, because surely if they'd been brought to some kind of execution chamber, she would have reacted differently. Not that he really thought Umberto would *kill* him. That wasn't how the old bastard operated. He preferred to come at people financially, because ruin was more fun.

Still, Pau didn't expect this to be *pleasant*, either way.

The man in black was waiting for them and the doors were open, so Pau took Leontina's arm and ushered her in with him to what he assumed was Umberto's questionable version of a throne room. It was a sitting room of sorts, but was done all in gold. Some of it real gold, he could see. It was a travesty of taste, but then, he supposed that was the point. It was so opulent, so over the top, that its only purpose had to be for Umberto to flatter himself with his own wealth.

After all, it wasn't *his* blood that built this castle. It hadn't been *his* ancestors who had tied themselves to this land, marking time with the fields they'd tilled and the villages they'd built. This castle had been built by nobility as a fortress many centuries ago in wars forgotten by most, and had fallen in and out of disrepair since. Umberto had divested the last remaining blood relative of that once-noble line of the last of his funds, self-respect, and possessions in one fell swoop.

Umberto had called it a business deal.

But like most of his deals, it had ruined everyone else involved.

This castle was a monument to the epic, soulless

greed of a man who took things and broke them simply because he could.

And this throne room was perhaps the ghastliest example of money failing to buy taste that Pau had ever seen.

It almost made him something like sad, as it suggested that Umberto was unworthy of the time and effort Pau had spent getting to this moment.

Almost.

But then, all the way on the other side of the room, was the little man himself. Umberto was not a tall or athletic man, and had not been one even in his youth. He was also not an attractive man. He was known to claim that he had a certain *charisma* that brought him women and acolytes and whatever else it was he desired, but that was what all rich, ugly men said.

It was always about money.

It took Pau a moment to note that all of Umberto's malevolent attention was not on him, but on his daughter.

"I see you've come crawling back as I knew you would," Umberto began, rising up from what looked like a gold-plated chaise to come charging toward Leontina—

Until he stopped short, wheezing in astonishment when he got closer.

Several things became immediately clear.

First, Umberto had clearly not been informed that it was Pau accompanying his runaway daughter. Second, the fact that said runaway daughter was visibly pregnant was clearly also a surprise.

And as she stood beside him, Pau could see that Leontina was doing something with her hand. She was making it look as if she was playing with her ring absently, but Pau rather doubted it. Because what she was doing made her ring catch the light and send it dancing all over this gleaming room, announcing their marriage without having to say it out loud.

"What the fuck is this?" shouted Umberto, his face going red and his eyes bugging out.

"Which part?" Pau asked, and he took pride in how even his voice was. How very nearly *bored* he sounded, because he could see how very little his lifelong enemy liked it. "Because I think you know what this is, old man."

Umberto looked from him to Leontina, and appeared to be very nearly shaking with rage. It seemed like a good start to Pau, though he made sure he kept close to Leontina. Very close, because Umberto always preyed on what he perceived as weakness first.

Leontina smiled at her father without a shred of fear. "I didn't care for your selection of suitors, Father," she told him in that cheerful voice of hers that Pau didn't like at all when it was directed at him. But he found he liked it fine today, aimed straight at her father. "So I went and found my own."

"You did not leave here long enough ago to come back fat with child!" Umberto was sputtering. He was staring at her belly and then he stepped in with a fist outstretched, as if he truly believed he might actually *strike* her.

As if he imagined that Pau would allow such a thing.

Much less the two men standing behind him.

Pau's men moved forward immediately, putting

themselves between Umberto and Leontina. Umberto stopped, and dropped his fist.

But Pau learned things about his wife in that moment, because she didn't so much as flinch. That smile didn't move from her face.

"Pau and I met at Giaco's wedding," she continued, as if there had been no interruption. As if her father's spike of rage didn't register with her. "I thought you would be pleased, Father. Haven't you always said you wanted to marry me off to a man of wealth and consequence that matches yours? I believe the good news is Pau's far exceeds yours. So this can only be an upgrade, correct?"

Umberto's face was getting redder and redder. Alarmingly red, in fact. His eyes were wild as he fixed them on Pau. "You… You…"

That was all he managed to get out, most of it a wheeze.

"Me," Pau agreed, his voice lethal. "What did you think? That you could really steal everything my father loved out from under him and nothing would come of it? That you would never answer for the things you do?"

"Your father was an idiot," Umberto bellowed. "He should have sold to me when he had the chance."

"Now you are nothing but an embarrassment," Pau said quietly. And distinctly, to make sure the old man heard him, and well. "A laughingstock in every circle you once imagined you ruled. How does that feel?"

Umberto's face was now approaching a worrisome crimson.

Pau did not stop. "Meanwhile, your daughter is mine," he said. "Wedded and bedded and carrying my child. Your legacy no longer exists, Umberto. It will stay in this tawdry room and tarnish as you do, until it is torn down and forgotten. Mine, on the other hand, grows deeper roots by the day. And let me assure you that Leontina and I will raise our son to know absolutely nothing about you."

"Over my dead body," Umberto shouted, and then he lunged in their direction—

But he never made it.

He never even reached Pau's waiting security guards. He lunged in their direction but tripped as he went, twisting in on himself and then falling heavily to the ground.

His head slammed into the marble floor.

Where he then lay, stiff and silent, for the length of a breath. Maybe two.

Maybe a small eternity as Pau and his men and Leontina all simply *stared* in the jarring silence.

But then the man in black let out a shout from behind them, and everything after that was chaos.

The staff came pouring in. There was panic all over the castle, there was an endless amount of rushing around, and ultimately they carried the old man out and loaded him on a helicopter staffed with paramedics to take him to the nearest hospital in Florence.

Pau was in the middle of things. He had Giaco on the phone the whole time, and it wasn't until he received word that Umberto had made it to the hospital and was declared stable that he realized he hadn't seen Leontina in a long while.

Since that moment they'd all stared at the old man crumpled on the floor—not a monster any longer, not a terror, not a Machiavellian villain. Just a breakable human who had hurt himself and fallen, subject to the rules of gravity and mortality like all the rest of them.

Pau still couldn't get his head around it, not really—but he ceased caring once he realized he didn't know where Leontina was.

His first thought was that she'd run again. And even as he thought that, he also wondered how he could blame her if she had. If he was her, he imagined he'd have made it to the border by now without so much as a glance back.

Being in this castle and watching the literal downfall of the wickedest man he'd ever known made his own behavior stand out to him, starkly.

And not with the honor he'd always believed he had on his side.

She had told him she loved him. And what had he done? He had acted no better than her father. Cold. Abrasive.

Could he blame her if she decided that she would be better off on her own?

He looked around the main hall, where there were still staff members rushing around, and whispering to each other. No doubt feeling a mixture of competing emotions tonight, because it didn't take much to discern that even Umberto's staff did not care much for him. Pau would be deeply surprised if they were even well compensated.

"Have you seen—" he began, when he caught the eye of one of the members of staff who had handled herself particularly well during all of this.

The woman studied him.

Then, "Come with me," she said, and started off so quickly that Pau didn't have time to confirm that they were talking about the same thing.

Still, he followed. He kept pace with the woman as she took him, bewilderingly, into what he assumed were the servants' quarters and then up sets of stairs that wound around behind the walls of the castle.

Several stories up, she led him out into a hallway that spoke to the castle's age and certainly had none of the questionable grandeur of the more public floors below.

She marched him down to the end of the hallway, stopped, and pointed at the door at the end.

Before he could ask her where the hell he was, and why, she disappeared again.

So Pau pushed open the door, not certain why his heart was pounding so hard in his chest, and stepped inside.

It was a bedchamber, though it looked to him like something out of medieval times. Everything was stone. The floors, the walls, the small, slitted windows. There was a canopied bed in the middle, a trunk at the end of the bed, a tapestry too faded to make out what might once have been on it and, more importantly to his eye, there was a large armchair in front of the fireplace.

Where, though no fire was lit, Leontina was sitting. With a pile of what looked like particularly weathered books in her lap.

He felt a deep sense of relief go through him, because she was here. She hadn't run. And on the heels of that, he felt something else. It was like a blow, but it lingered, making his heart ache.

So much he found he needed to press his palm there against his chest.

Pau didn't think she'd looked up when he walked in, but when Leontina spoke, it was clear that she knew exactly who had come in.

"I thought that if I read the books in your house, I would get to know you," she said quietly. "That I'd be able to figure you out based on who you read, and how well read the pages were. That the clues to who you are would be pressed between the pages, waiting to be uncovered."

She did turn then, and he couldn't place the expression on her face. It seemed remote. Possibly even something like sad.

He felt his heart kick in again, harder.

But Leontina kept going.

"I finally realized why." She picked up one of the books in her lap and he realized it was a journal. "My mother left me these when she died. Her whole collection." She shook her head. "I was quite young. I never really knew her. My father liked to tell me that she did not wish to know me, so as you can imagine, I found these journals something of a lifeline. And I excavated them for signs of her."

She looked down at the journal in her hand. "But words on a page, even if they are direct thoughts, can only be part of the story. And with you, I only had the books you read, not your thoughts on them. I read as many of them as I could since I arrived in Spain. I treated it like a job, with a deadline." Now, finally, she looked at him, her jade green eyes grave. "But what do I really know about you, in the end?"

Pau didn't like where this was going. "Leontina. This has been a very emotional day."

"So you can only have emotions when they're negative, is that it?" she asked.

She smiled when she said it, but it wasn't her real smile, and in any case he felt her words like a wallop across the face. He was surprised he remained standing.

"That's neither true nor fair," he managed to get out, though he wasn't at all sure he wasn't lying himself.

"My mother killed herself," Leontina told him softly. "I think everyone knows that, but the story is always told to make it seem as if it was an accident. As if maybe she didn't mean to do it. Or maybe she was too overwrought, too mentally ill, too…*something* to know better."

"Your father is stable," Pau told her. "If you're worried about losing another parent, however substandard he might be."

She studied him for a moment. "Today I realized something. I know my brother never read these journals, because if he had, he would know better than to think she simply effected the only escape she could. She did do that, don't misunderstand me. But it wasn't *only* that she wanted to escape my father." She held up one of the journals. "She wanted to cause him pain in the only way she could. Not that it would hurt his feelings, of course, but it would embarrass him. Whether people thought she was weak or thought she hated him that much, either way, it would embarrass him that she took control like that, and so publicly. That consumed her. I think that's what revenge does. It consumes, then it corrodes."

"Leontina."

She set the journal down on the arm of the chair and fixed him with that grave gaze again. Her hand snuck over her belly, though she didn't look away. "But I want you to know that I've already made a vow to our son. No matter what happens, no matter who we hate or how wretched we think our enemies are, he comes first. And I intend to hold this vow, Pau. No matter what."

It was how calmly she was saying these things, he thought. It felt like an indictment. It felt as if she was stripping him naked and baring parts of him that had never seen the light to her gaze. To his own gaze.

Revenge consumes, then corrodes. That was what she'd said.

He could not help but wonder how he'd convinced himself that keeping his focus steady and never, ever stopping this thing no matter how complicated it got between the two of them was a *good* thing. How he'd been so certain that his father would applaud this from beyond the grave, if he could.

When the truth, as Pau knew too well, was that his father had been consumed and corroded in equal measure, though it wasn't revenge that he'd chased. It was land and legacy and the perfect bottle of wine.

Standing here in Umberto's castle, Pau found himself feeling far from victorious. He was forced to wonder if he—and his father—were more like the man who had dominated both of their lives, and ended Bernat's, than Pau wanted to admit.

Even thinking it made him feel ill.

"I have only ever had one enemy in my life," Pau told her, feeling that pounding in his chest again and an accompanying urgency he wasn't sure he could explain. "And I'll be honest with you, Leontina. Watching him effect his own undoing today did not exactly assuage my father's death the way I thought it would."

Saying that out loud made him feel…worse, perhaps. Messier, certainly.

"I hate being back here," she replied after a moment. "If I'm honest, I wouldn't mind at all if this place burned to the ground. I'd likely celebrate. Yet coming back here has made things clear to me, at last."

He wasn't sure why that made him want to panic. "Leontina."

She ignored him.

"I will not disappear from my life," she told him then, her voice strong. Sure. Her gaze intent on his. "If you don't like the fact that I'm in love with you, that's your problem. I will not diminish myself for you or anyone else. Ever."

She stood up then, setting the journals aside, and he saw that she was breathing rapidly, too. He wanted to go and put his mouth on the pulse in her neck. He wanted to get his hands on her any way he could.

He *wanted her* and that had changed everything.

But she wasn't finished. "And I'll tell you something else, Pau. I'm not going to raise our baby on revenge. On hatred. On nasty little plots that take decades and end in a sick, twisted old man on the floor with a banged-up head and no one to care about him but staff members he treats terribly." Her eyes blazed, a wild, bright green. "My baby will be raised with hope. Love. And as much joy as he can handle."

He said her name again, but it came out a whisper. A wish. A kind of prayer.

Leontina did not look away from him. He wasn't sure she blinked. "If we can't have that with you, Pau, that will break my heart. But I will leave you too if I have to."

And he opened his mouth to tell her that none of that would be necessary, but he couldn't seem to get the words out. All those pressure points that had been pressing on him caved him in. Because it was suddenly clear to him that all the structures inside him that held him in place, that made him who he was…crumbled.

Into so much ash and dust, just like that.

CHAPTER ELEVEN

LEONTINA COULD FEEL her heartbeat going wild inside her. She couldn't tell if she was terrified or determined or some mix of both, and all of it seemed to be wrapped up in how much she didn't want to say any of the things she'd just said to him.

But it was all true. She'd felt like a kind of warrior queen walking into the front hall of the monastery in Spain today. She'd felt powerful and she'd known that it got to him. That she did. That her silence worked its way beneath his skin.

She'd been able to ride that wave all the way here. It had held even after she'd walked into the castle, finding it as unpleasant and oppressive as ever. It had been a struggle not to run for one of her hiding places. But Pau had been at her side and the truth was, Leontina found she really didn't mind the idea of sticking it to her father.

He'd certainly had it coming.

The reality of that moment, on the other hand, she'd found had made her feel hollow.

After Umberto had first looked as if he'd meant to strike her belly—her child—and had then thrown himself through the air in her direction as if he dearly wished to do her—*his* child—bodily harm, she'd understood what that hollowness was.

A kind of grief. It tasted like despair, but it wasn't. It was a mourning.

For the little girl she'd been here who had learned how to hide because solitude and concealing herself was an act of love, one she showed herself, and it was all she got. For the young woman who had been told all the ways she could be *useful*, but was never valued as anything but an object to trade at a market. Little more than a trinket who mattered only if some man could be convinced her price was worth paying.

It wasn't like these things were new. Leontina had been quite aware of what her life was all along. What was different was her. Or more accurately, the baby she carried inside her.

Leontina had understood in a flash, while her father lay in a heap on the floor, his face red and his head bloodied from the impact, that the things she had put up with, the life she'd lived, the entire toxic swamp of this place and her father and everything that came with it were going to end right here.

She wished she could care about her father's welfare, but she couldn't.

What she knew was that she would never let that man anywhere near her child. Not only that, *her* child would never experience the things she had as a girl. Her son was already loved and adored beyond reason and Leontina hadn't even met him yet. And her son would only hide if he was playing a game. She could feel the sheer intensity of how much she loved him and what she would do to protect him and how she would make certain that even if no one else in the world loved her boy, he would know that she did. He would *know*.

And as all of that had rushed through her, she'd known that she needed to be done with these schemes and plots, these revenge scenarios and where they led.

Because it was always to the same place, wasn't it?

Her father had tripped and fallen on the cold stone floor and no one had rushed to him. He had done nothing but bully and plot his whole life, and this was where it ended.

She loved Pau. The more she accepted that, the more she was sure that it had been there from the moment she'd met his gaze. From the moment she'd felt the intensity he carried within him, before she'd felt how he expressed it.

Like she had been waiting for him all her life and it was worth it, to be locked away in a castle all that time, if it meant she got to have him after all. Leontina thought she would dream about the time they'd spent together for the rest of her life.

But there was no way in hell that she would raise her child in this mess. No possible way.

And she'd said these things to him here, in the castle, where she could hide from almost anything but the reality of her life here. She'd said it so she couldn't think better of it and let years pass, only to end up trapped in exactly the place she knew she didn't want to go.

The truth was she expected Pau to go arctic again, and walk away.

But instead, he went pale.

Then suddenly, everything about him *blazed*.

Pau moved toward her so swiftly that she didn't have time to react. Then his hands were on her upper arms, holding her to him. His face was so close to hers that she almost thought she could taste him, and there was a look she'd never seen before in his eyes.

She found she was holding her breath.

"I will not live without you, Leontina," he hurled at her. "I will not do it. And you will not raise this child— *my child*—without me, either."

Of all the things she'd thought he might say, it wasn't that. She'd thought maybe he would sternly lecture her about legacies. Or the papers they'd signed. Or the promises they'd made, none having anything to do with spite or love or anything but the kind of coolheaded, emotionless agreements that Pau Calixto was known for.

But she couldn't let herself believe him. She might have been willing to risk herself because her heart told her she *needed* to, but this wasn't about her. It couldn't be.

"I will not raise a child with you in a cauldron of spite," she shot right back at him.

"There is no cauldron," he retorted, and his fingers dug into her shoulders as he spoke, but she didn't mind. She thought that here, now, she was finally seeing the real Pau. "I thought that this would be a victory, after all the plans I'd made. I thought that all of this would feel different once it happened. Once he knew. But we got here, and he was just the same tiny, little man he's always been, and the only thing I care about is you."

That made her heart stutter, but she shook her head.

"I've seen no evidence to support that. In your books or anywhere else."

"*I married you*," he thundered at her. "I sought you out, allowed you to seduce me, and did everything in my power to get you with child, woman. What did you think was happening?"

"I *let* you seduce me," she countered. "And I *wanted* a baby. I needed a reason that you would have to marry me, and I knew you would if there was a child involved, because that's the kind of man you are. I never expected to fall in love with you, but here we are." She made a face. "Or here *I* am, I suppose I should say."

Pau made a low noise, like some kind of growl.

"How would I know if I was in love with you or not?" he gritted out at her, his grip intense but his gaze even more so. "How would I know what love is? There was my mother, who loved only my father, but he barely saw her and she left him. There was my father, who loved only the land, the vines, the Calixto legacy, and it as good as killed him. What am I to think love is?"

Leontina felt breathless. "You could start—"

But he shushed her by pulling her even closer to him.

"And then there's you," Pau said. "Sister to the only human being on this planet that I would tell you I actually do love. My only friend. The only man I trust. And I betrayed him, because I decided that you were the only revenge worth taking on a man I shouldn't have cared about at all. Because what is Umberto Tavian to me? I own him. I ruined him. He's nothing—and I am a man of figures and plans, Leontina. I do not *feel*. I do not *pine*. I made myself into a human spreadsheet for a reason."

But his hands moved, then. One to the swell of her belly, the other to carefully cup her cheek as he moved even closer. "So all I can think is that all of this time, all of these wild and impossible *feelings*—it's all been about you."

Leontina liked that. She more than liked it.

Still. "You would have tried to seduce me at that wedding no matter who I was, as long as I was his daughter," she said, though she pressed her cheek deeper into his palm.

"I would have," he agreed, his voice low. "But I wouldn't be obsessed. I wouldn't suffer from these sleepless nights, unable to think or rest or do anything at all but *pine* over you. I wouldn't see you wherever I go. I wouldn't dream of you when I'm lucky enough to actually fall asleep. I sweat you out. I bury myself in my work. I lament you. I curse you. And yet none of it is any good. You're still here." He moved his hand from her belly to his chest and thumped himself right where his heart beat. "You're *right here*, Leontina, and I can't get you out. I don't know how."

He sounded tortured. Leontina slid her hand over his, the one he held to her cheek, and that made his breath come out of him in a sigh.

"If that's not love," Pau said to her, his voice low and his eyes dark, "then it is some terrible disease that is killing me as I stand here. Either way, it's your fault."

And as declarations went, Leontina thought that this one was the finest she'd ever heard. All this from a man who hardly knew *how* to feel? She felt as if he'd written her sonnets.

She found herself smiling, her cheeks were damp,

and as she moved closer to him and slid her hands over that tight jaw of his, she kissed him.

Once, then again.

"I don't think you're dying," she told him, not able to keep the laughter out of her voice. "These are your feelings, Pau. Welcome."

"What I *feel* is more like cardiac arrest," he said, frowning, but when she moved to place her hand over his heart, he covered it with his.

"I bet it's not," she said, unable to stop smiling at him. "Though I suppose there's only one way to find out."

"Is there a test for this?" he asked, sounding grumpy and ruined, wounded, and hers.

That was the part that mattered. *Hers*.

"There is," Leontina said, and wound her arms around his neck. "It's called happily ever after, Pau. It's forever, at a minimum. I guess we'll have to see how it goes."

Then she took her husband by the hand, led him to her childhood bed where nothing of interest had ever happened, and properly seduced him, at last.

Fully aware that as she did it, he seduced her right back.

And what did it matter who seduced who, when in the end, they found themselves tangled up with each other and wound too tight to ever let go.

So they never did.

CHAPTER TWELVE

UMBERTO DID NOT die that night, but he was severely diminished.

Leontina declared that it was a fitting punishment and Pau found he agreed.

When the old man really did die, only a few years later, his funeral was a bleak affair. Giaco came with Ivy. Pau went with Leontina. There were none of the old acolytes and vultures, which made it a quiet affair. They put the old man in the ground in the mausoleum of a castle he had loved so much, and Pau was fairly certain that the only reason any of them went was to make sure the man who had been an outsize presence in all their lives was well and truly buried.

And just as he had told Umberto on the last night they'd spoken, once he was gone, they rarely thought of him again.

Because life outside the old man's greed and all the misery he had caused was *good*. It was far more interesting. It was joyful. It was sometimes hard, even dark upon occasion, but there were always constellations to guide the way when the night wore on too long. There was always a reason to hold on until morning.

Dawn always came, and Pau knew it would, because he could see it in his wife's beautiful smile, free of pretense now, warm and giving and *his*.

He liked to tell her that he would always see her. That she could never disappear, because he would always find her.

"Remember," he would say, "I am the one who noticed you when you wore sacks and made your face blank and strange."

She would always laugh and press herself against him. "*I* saw *you*, Pau. That's what made the difference."

And though he did not plan to admit it for another few decades or so, he rather thought she was right.

Their son was born that first winter. He came crashing into the world and into Pau's heart with a love so intense and so vast it was almost funny that he had ever imagined he could avoid it. That he could somehow hold himself back from love.

He stopped trying.

Instead, he continued the tradition of family dinners, always moving from one room in the monastery to another.

"When will you pick your favorite dining room?" Leontina asked him when their son was a toddler and they were soon to bring their first daughter into the world.

"Never," he told her. "I want every night to feel as much like an adventure as every day with you does, my love."

And as the children grew, they took turns choosing new places for the family dinners too, until it became a hallmark of the Calixto family—only this time, steeped in love and laughter, affection and fun.

Both Pau and Giaco were deeply committed to building families that were nothing like the ones they'd grown up in. So as the two old friends expanded their families, they made certain that the cousins were together as much as possible. They got to watch their children become as close as siblings ought to be. They got to watch them play and laugh, grow bored and come up with imaginative ways to cure it, and live out the actual childhoods neither one of them had really had.

They got to watch as their wives—former stepsisters—became the kind of deep, true friends that Pau and Giaco had always been for each other.

As the years passed, Leontina and Ivy became more like sisters.

They renovated the castle and sold it, vowing that none of their babies would set foot on such poisoned ground. As one big family, they spent summers together, in a sprawling chateau in the hills above the gleaming beaches of the Côte d'Azur that sat in a wild estate that felt as if it was centuries removed from the concerns of the world.

Pau and his best friend turned brother made sure it stayed that way.

They spent the summers without staff, cooking their meals and shopping in the markets and teaching their children how to fend for themselves. How to recognize peace and how to fight for it despite the demands the world would make of them thanks to their family.

And when their oldest daughter got married on that same estate years later, the first of all their children to do it, Pau was there when Ivy reached over and took Leontina's hand.

"I don't know if you remember," Ivy said, "but you told me long ago that you would be the family for me that I couldn't have because my mother wasn't there at my wedding. And I told you that I would do the same for you, but you insisted on marrying Pau in secret." She smiled, though her eyes were shining. "So now I've taken it upon myself to act as the mother of the mother of the bride, in whatever capacity I can, so it will be almost as if both of our mothers are here."

Leontina took Ivy's hands and didn't make the slightest effort to contain her tears. "I think they are here," she whispered. "Just look at our babies, all grown up. I know they're here, Ivy. They've been with us all along."

Pau raised his children to respect and honor the Calixto family legacy, but he never let it crush them. He brought them to Australia to visit their grandmother, and didn't correct her when she told her stories—not many of them flattering toward the father he still loved, but could see more critically now. They were her stories about her time in Spain with her former husband. She could tell them as she wished, and he wasn't afraid to answer any questions his sons and daughters might have about the things she said.

What kept him up in the night sometimes was worrying that if they weren't exposed to enough alternate stories, they might end up the way he almost had. A blind man rushing toward an empty victory with no access to his heart.

He taught them to love first, because all things followed from there.

Maybe this was why, as the years ripened and their family grew with daughters and sons-in-law and grand-babies of their own, it only seemed to get sweeter.

And at the end of every day, he and his beautiful wife would find themselves together in the bed they always shared, where they would tangle themselves up, make each other whole, and sleep pressed close together.

Like joy made real.

* * * * *

Get up to 4 Free Books!

We'll send you 2 free books from each series you try
PLUS a free Mystery Gift.

Both the **Harlequin Presents** and **Harlequin Medical Romance** series feature exciting stories of passion and drama.

YES! Please send me 2 FREE novels from Harlequin Presents or Harlequin Medical Romance and my FREE gift (gift is worth about $10 retail). I may cancel anytime by emailing ReaderServiceInfo@Harlequin.com or by calling 1-800-873-8635. If I don't cancel, I will receive 6 brand-new larger-print novels every month and be billed just $7.19 each in the U.S., or $7.99 each in Canada, or 4 brand-new Harlequin Medical Romance Larger-Print books every month and be billed just $7.19 each in the U.S. or $7.99 each in Canada. That's a savings of 20% off the cover price! It's quite a bargain! Shipping and handling is just 75¢ per book in the U.S. and $1.75 per book in Canada.* I understand that accepting the free books and gift places me under no obligation to buy anything—they are mine to keep for free no matter what I decide.

Choose one:

☐ **Harlequin Presents Larger-Print** (176/376 BPA G3CD)

☐ **Harlequin Medical Romance** (171/371 BPA G3CD)

☐ **Or Try Both!** (176/376 & 171/371 BPA G3CE)

____
Name (please print)

____
Address   Apt. #

____
City   State/Province   Zip/Postal Code

Email: Please check this box ☐ if you would like to receive newsletters and promotional emails from Harlequin Enterprises ULC and its affiliates. You can unsubscribe anytime.

> **Mail to the Harlequin Reader Service:**
> **IN U.S.A.:** P.O. Box 1341, Buffalo, NY 14240-8531
> **IN CANADA:** P.O. Box 603, Fort Erie, Ontario L2A 5X3

Want to explore our other series or interested in ebooks? Visit www.ReaderService.com or call 1-800-873-8635.

*Terms and prices subject to change without notice. Prices do not include sales taxes, which will be charged (if applicable) based on your state or country of residence. Canadian residents will be charged applicable taxes. Offer not valid in Quebec. This offer is limited to one order per household. Books received may not be as shown. Not valid for current subscribers to the Harlequin Presents or Harlequin Medical Romance series. All orders subject to approval. Credit or debit balances in a customer's account(s) may be offset by any other outstanding balance owed by or to the customer. Please allow 4 to 6 weeks for delivery. Offer available while quantities last.

Your Privacy — Your information is being collected by Harlequin Enterprises ULC, operating as Harlequin Reader Service. For a complete summary of the information we collect, how we use this information and to whom it is disclosed, please visit our privacy notice located at https://corporate.harlequin.com/privacy-notice. Notice to California Residents—Under California law, you have specific rights to control and access your data. For more information on these rights and how to exercise them, visit https://corporate.harlequin.com/california-privacy. For additional information for residents of other U.S. states that provide their residents with certain rights with respect to personal data, visit https://corporate.harlequin.com/other-state-residents-privacy-rights.

HPHM2603